More than the Sparrows

Joanne C. Jensen

PublishAmerica
Baltimore

ISBN: 978-1-60749-766-0 (softcover)
ISBN: 978-1-4489-1795-2 (hardcover)
PUBLISHED BY PUBLISHAMERICA, LLLP ◆
www.publishamerica.com
Baltimore

Printed in the United States of America

To the memory of John Derek, my precious son.

To my wonderful family for all their help to me in my writing: My husband John who edits my work; Holly the artist who designed the cover of my book; Melodie who urges me on and John Derek who inspires me from His Home in Heaven above. Thank you family.

More than the Sparrows

Chapter One

Ballymore Farm spread out over the green of Northern Irelands' eminence and dales a half day or so journey from Londonderry. The imposing manor house was set high on a bluff that overlooked the river Foyle. Ballymore Farm had been in the ownership of the same family for a hundred years and more.

This morning the mist hung like a blue veil over the sleepy valley. Golden rays of sunlight sparkled with glittering radiance across the dewdrops on the upper meadow. The air was cool and fresh and fused with the scent of the sea not far away.

It was a blithe and lovely morning, but young Shalaghs' thoughts were on none of these. No, she had risen early, much too excited for sleep. This is the day they would travel to Derry and visit Aunt Hala and Uncle Will. How Shalagh adored these pleasant excursions. They as a family would leave early this morning and could possibly arrive there in time for a late lunch.

"Are you awake, Tara?" questioned Shalagh softly so as not to disturb her sister if she was still asleep.

When Shalagh received no response, she repeated the question, only, this time a bit louder and with greater emphasis.

"No, I am not awake, and I am too tired too open my eyes. Go away!" came the sound of a muffled voice from under the soft white comforter.

Tara moved slightly in the bed on the other side of the room. The sun was now filling the room with light and a gentle breeze stirred the frilly white curtains at the windows. Only a few dark curls escaped and lay across the smooth surface of Tara's pillow.

Thump! A pillow suddenly flew through the air from the other bed and landed on top of Tara.

"Go away," moaned Tara, "let me sleep".

"Well, if you are not awake, I will wake you," giggled Shalagh as she moved quickly across the room and crept upon the bed of her younger sister. Tara's dark head roused from under the warm coverlet as Shalagh jumped about upon the bed.

"Shalagh!" shrieked the younger sister jumping from the rolling bed. "Have you no mercy? I am not a morning person and I did not sleep well last night. I had a terrible dream." She reached crossly for her robe, which she threw about her trim young shoulders. It was cold in the room even though it was early August.

"Why do you keep the windows wide open at night? Even when it rains you do that and it is too cold in here," complained Tara. She sat back down on the bed and drew her slim legs under her to keep warm.

Tara had just celebrated her fifteenth birthday a few days ago. Only eleven months apart, yet the appearance of the sisters were greatly similar. Shalagh's hair was somewhat lighter, but still each had long silky locks that fell to their waist. Shalagh's eyes were as blue as her sister's and papa often mistook the girls for each other. They had inherited their mother's beauty and their father's indomitable spirit. Mama said it would have been easier to have triplets as Caleb, their older brother, was only a year and a few days older than Shalagh.

Although the girls shared each other's dark beauty, their characters were much different.

Shalagh had a great ambition to learn and was at the top of her class at the academy for girls attended by both she and Tara. Shalagh appeared to be highly intelligent and her academic achievements had caused some to judge her as brilliant. This judgment she scoffed at, explaining it away with how hard and long she studied to accomplish these results.

Tara was equally perceptive but seemed prone to dream. It wasn't that she meant to, yet much too often her thoughts wandered away from the dull sounds of the classroom and did not return quickly enough to grasp the depths of the subject matter. Tara tried to concentrate, but it was not understood until much later that due to a childhood illness, Tara had been left with a hearing disability. She heard only parts of what was said by the instructors. She herself was unaware of her predicament, as she had no memory of hearing any other way. With great intent she would attempt to listen to the instructors' droning voice, but more often than not would tire of it and her thoughts would wander away. Soon she would be caught up in some adventure of her own imagination, her mind returning too late to learn the lessons taught that day. Still her classmates adored her and although Tara's instructors strongly admonished her, they could not help but agree that she was a fair and normal child in appearance and so they judged her only to be lazy.

Many years later Shalagh wrote in her diary that it was my sister who had a brilliant mind. Had anyone known or had been able to help with her disability, Tara would have achieved much sooner than myself as her great accomplishments proved later in life.

A knock sounded on the door of the bedroom.

"Girls are you awake?" questioned Mama's voice.

"Yes, yes we are," Shalagh assured her.

"Come down then for breakfast. Your father and brothers have finished eating," explained Mama as she opened the door to the sunny room.

Mama carried baby Carly in her arms. Rosy cheeked Willy followed close behind her and bounced merrily into the room. He was gleefully excited because he was to join the family on the trip today. He clapped his chubby hands and danced around the room, his blond curls bouncing around his cherub like face.

"Willy go too, Willy go too," he shouted happily.

"Oh sweet Willy, come and give me a morning kiss," laughed Tara. She had now really come awake.

Willy ran to the bed and planted a kiss on Tara's waiting cheek just as Shalagh reached down and plucked up the chubby three-year old in her arms. She laughingly danced out the door, down the hall and to the stairs. Willy gave no resistance, but screamed in delight.

"Willy and I are going to beat you to the breakfast table, Tara," she laughed. Willy thinking it great fun echoed the words back at Tara.

"Sala and Willy beat you, Tara. We will eat all the food. Hurry, hurry, Sala," he yelled in childish glee.

There was plenty of food left when Tara arrived at the table. There was never a lack of anything for the Frizzle family of Ballymore Farm. The land was rich and fertile, some of the best in Northern Ireland. The family grew surplus crops of wheat, flax and potatoes and Ballymore Farm prospered greatly. The dairy herd was the best anywhere about. The servants were well cared for and their quarters' comfortable. There was enty for all at Ballymore and the manor house was a joyful place in which to live.

It is true that Robert Frizzle (papa) had not been accepted by the family when he had begun courting Taryn (mama). He and his brother Will were Catholic you know and the family were all good Presbyterians. Oh, it was bad for awhile, especially when added to everything, Will began to court Hala, Taryn's older sister. Robert and Will loved the two sisters so much that they converted to the Episcopalian faith, stating that was the best they could do. It seemed to work and another word was never said about it. Robert and Taryn, Will and Hala were married in a double wedding ceremony in the parlor of Ballymore in the year 1828. Robert and Taryn chose to live on the farm at Ballymore, where they raised their family. Will and Hala made their home in Derry where the brothers owned a linen mill. The families were very close and traveled back and forth on a regular basis.

So today it was a happy group that started off for Londonderry that early summer morning. The carriage was crowded with Papa and Mama, Willy, the two girls and Dylan, who was thirteen. Caleb the oldest declared it was much too crowded and rode with the driver up front. Baby Carly being less than a year old was too young to enjoy the trip so with many kisses and hugs was left at home in the good hands of the long time family nanny. Still Mama worried and looked sad until the merriment of the family caught up with her. She finally joined with the rest in singing and laughing as they jostled along the road to Derry.

The ride was pleasant and Shalagh carried a quiet excitement in her heart even though she joined readily in the singing and merriment. Shalagh had met a young man in the spring when she had visited Hala and Uncle Will. He was there with his mother, a friend of Aunt Hala from England. Shalagh longed to hear any news about him. Secretly, she hoped he might be visiting again.

The singing had stopped now and Papa had taken up the telling of one of his stories. He could keep you spellbound with his tales of the wee people or spirit apparitions. Papa had been raised in an environment of great superstition and still clung to some of the old beliefs. Mama would have none of it and her strong Presbyterian upbringing completely eliminated the supernatural people and such. Mama believed in God and the Bible as did Papa, still he could not completely separate himself from some of the old ways. Anyway, Mama loved Papa so much that she would allow him to tell his fairy stories as long as the children knew they were not true.

"Papa, please don't tell about the horse riding ghost," pleaded Tara looking very upset.

"No, Robert, we are not going to speak of friendly apparitions. We are going to enjoy the day," admonished Mama while patting Tara gently on the knee. Mama knew how some of Papa's stories frightened Tara.

Papa obliged happily. He had no desire to cause any problems and kept the mood lighthearted with his funny jaunty tales.

They made good time and arrived a little early at aunt and uncle's fine house in Derry.

Aunt Hala was waiting for them in the grand style with which she did everything. She was Mama's only sibling and two years her senior. She and Uncle Will had no children until later in life. They were joyfully happy when they were blessed with a little girl, Rylie, now five and a baby boy a year later. They called him Brin. They were the joy and heart of their parents' lives.

"Oh, come in, come in," greeted Aunt Hala throwing open the front door. Aunt Hala was lovely as usual, dressed in a soft flowing gown of a linen material. One could truthfully say that Aunt Hala was a beautiful woman, not only in person, in every way. It would not have mattered whether she was rich or poor her disposition was always one of happiness, as she was loved by everyone.

Rylie and Bryn joined in the greeting. After everyone had been acknowledged they followed Aunt Hala into the breakfast room. It was a bright sunny room with the windows wide open. The table was spread with delicious food and dainties.

"Please be seated," said Aunt Hala. "Come, Willy, we have set a little table for you and Brin here by the window.

The two little boys sat down together at a small child's table placed near the sunny window of the room. Only a year apart in age, the boys loved to play together. They seemed to have a language of their own.

"I knew that Rylie would not settle for anything but to sit between Tara and Shalagh at the table," laughed Aunt Hala.

The family had just settled at the table when Uncle Will came in.

"Well, hello Will," greeted Papa. "I didn't know if we would see you until later today. I was coming over to the mill myself after lunch was over.

"That would be good if you did," nodded Uncle Will. There are some things I would like to go over with you.

"Now, we are not going to talk about business at lunch," smiled Aunt Hala as she graciously poured tea.

Will gave her a loving look of admiration as she passed him.

"Not another word," he said smiling at her sweetly.

Papa had traded his partnership in the linen mills outright to Uncle Will a year before in exchange for Aunt Hala's right to

Ballymore. It was a happy and mutual agreement. Ballymore Farms were so productive that Papa had no time for the linen mills and Aunt Hala had no time for the farm. Shalagh wondered why Uncle wished to speak with Papa about the mill seeing he had nothing to do with it anymore.

After lunch Papa went with Uncle Will to the mill and the rest of the family spent a delightful day entertained by Aunt Hala and the children.

Papa did not return until much later than expected. Dinner was over and Uncle Will did not come with him. When he finally arrived, Papa ate a quick and silent meal and hardly spoke on the way home. Mama and Aunt Hala seemed worried and hugged each other with a great embrace when the family left for Ballymore. Shalagh was certain they were crying, but no one else seemed to notice so she said nothing.

It was late that same night that Shalagh and Tara were awakened from their sleep.

"I don't care what you say, you are robbers and thieves," Papa was yelling at someone.

The voices were coming from the study just below the girl's bedroom.

"You will take our offer or else," sounded an unfamiliar threatening voice.

"I won't do it! I'll fight you!" roared Papa. "I'll fight you to the death! Thieves! That is what you are nothing but thieves."

Shalagh ran to the bedroom door and pulled it open just as Mama came down the all. Mama put her finger to her lips and motioned for the girls to stay in their room.

"There are other ways," sounded another voice even more menacing than the first.

"My brother has no right to this land, the mills or anything else," yelled Papa. "Now, get out! Get out and don't come back!"

Mama pushed her way into the girl's room and shut the door.
"What is it Mama. What is wrong?" cried Tara.
"It is nothing," said Mama. "Papa will handle it. It is just some dealings between businessmen. I am sorry they got a little loud and woke you. Go back to sleep now. It would be best if papa did not know that you overheard," she suggested.
"But, Mama, why is Papa mad at Uncle Will?" questioned Shalagh. They have always loved and respected each other.
"Papa will take care of everything. He always does," Mama assured them. "He isn't angry at Uncle Will. It will all work out. Now, go to sleep." Then, making sure they were back in bed, she kissed them and left, shutting the door behind her.
"I have never heard Papa so angry," whispered Shalagh.
"Me either," declared Tara. "What do you think happened between him and Uncle Will and who are these men who came here tonight?"
"I don't know," said Shalagh. "We were all so happy this morning and now everything is in a state of confusion."
There was no more noise or shouting and finally the girls drifted off to sleep.

Chapter Two

No one ever knew for sure what really happen on the following morning. Papa rose early and went out into the fields to hunt. When he did not return by noon, Mama sent one of the help to look for him. They found him in the pasture slumped over his gun. From all appearances it would seem that he had shot himself. The authorities believed that he had been despondent over his finances and had ended his own life.

The family could not accept that and did not believe it was true. Papa was fully persuaded that it was a mortal sin in God's sight to take your own life. He would never have done that. However his death was ruled a suicide and no further investigation was ever pursued.

A message was sent off to Hala and Will but for some unknown and mystifying reason they did not come.

Before Papa was even buried, the bank adjusters converged upon Mama. The Plantation of Ballymore Farm had been given as a grant to the Boyd family generations ago. It was given to Aunt Hala and Mama by their parents Grandma and Grandpa Boyd. Mama knew little about running the plantation. She left everything up to Papa while she cared for the family and the house. It seemed that Papa had severe and disturbing financial problems. The day of Papa's funeral the bank adjusters went through everything in the manor house.

"What have you done to my house?" cried Mama after returning from the church. "You have no right to be here," she screamed at the adjusters.

They explained that they had every right and that because Papa was so badly in debt he had sold Ballymore. Everything, including the house and the stock, were a part of the estate that had to be sold. Papers and signed documents were produced as proof. All moneys had gone to payoff the debts.

The adjusters finally left leaving Mama in a state of panic. Caleb begged her to let him go to Derry and bring back Uncle Will. Mama was far too distraught to let him go, fearing that something terrible would happen to him.

The very next day an officer of the law came to remove the family from their home. He was touched by their plight. Realizing there were small children in the family and with no where to go he gave them permission to stay in the sheepherder's cottage on the edge of the plantation. The cottage was well over three miles from the manor house. The caretaker who was sent by the new owner to manage Ballymore was unaware of the small, unnoticed structure. The cottage set back from the road and was almost hidden from view by thick shrubbery.

Mama found herself disgraced and in total poverty. The church and those who she called friends were either unable or not willing to help. She could not understand why her dear sister did not come to their aid. Mama overcome with grief and despair collapsed. Losing Papa of itself had been more grief than Mama could bear. Their love and commitment to each other was one not often seen. Yes, she would have followed him to the ends of the earth and beyond, and so she did. Before the snows of November Mama joined him on the joyous shore of the Promised Land above. She died of a broken heart for she was not ill.

The struggle for survival was forced upon Caleb, Shalagh and Tara while Dylan did all he could to help.

The unprecedented cold and snow of the winters of 1846 and 1847 had brought great suffering and despair upon the people of Ireland. Famine and sickness were spreading with death dealing relentlessness. The homeless, destitute and starving were to be found everywhere. There were workhouses for the poor, but they were overcrowded and filled with disease. It was almost a death sentence to go there.

With the loss of their parents, their home and all finances Shalagh and her sister and brothers found themselves in the same dire circumstances as the poor. They were without resources to care for themselves. Until a short time ago they had known only the sheltering protective care of honorable and respected Christian parents. Now they were alone in a strange world-a frightening world-a land caught up in the talons of death's cruel grip.

Caleb and Dylan, the two boys, picked up what work they could by cleaning the stables at Ballymore. However, the pay was practically nothing and hard to come by. Food was scarce and becoming almost nonexistent. There was little to burn for fuel. Still they clung to each other and would not give up hope. The months after their parent's death went by slowly. The cottage gave them some protection from the cold and would-be thieves and danger. They thanked God for it. As yet no one had come to evict them, but they were ever fearful that they might soon be found.

This morning had begun with overcast skies and mist, but

the bitter cold had moved in later in the day. All day Shalagh had desperately searched the barren fields in hope of finding some food, but the basket that dangled from her slender arm was empty. Shalagh had gone far in search for food and now it had begun to snow.

She pulled her scarf more snugly about her head. All attempts to push back strands of hair that had fallen across her forehead were futile. Her hands were too cold and numb. The late winter wind swirled around her slight form and punished her tattered shawl with an icy vengeance. Particles of dirt mixed with snow and ice stung her ash white face. This provoked her eyes to smart and water, which blurred her vision. The shoes on her feet were shredded and held together with rags and offered little protection from the rough frozen sod. The pain in her feet caused her to grimace with every step. She could travel no further.

"It is useless," she whispered, accepting defeat. "There is not a scrap of food to be found anywhere.

"I am so cold," the girl shivered as she accepted the dismal hopelessness of her situation and began to retrace her steps toward home.

Moving blindly against the wind, her sight obscured, she stumbled and fell face down upon the cold ground. Softly weeping, Shalagh struggled to raise herself to a sitting position. Her long dark hair fell loose from the scarf, which had now slipped to her shoulders. Her bare hands were scraped and bleeding from the fall, but she hardly noticed.

"I must get up," she whispered now trying to rise. "Tara will be worried." But instead she slumped back unto the ground, too weak to stand.

Darkness was fast moving in. She attempted once more to stand upon her feet but she could not. She longed for the company of Dylan her younger brother who often helped her in search of the fields.

This morning however, he had gone with Caleb, the eldest to the stables of Ballymore.

For the sum of her sixteen years of life, Shalagh had embraced a fervent and unquestionable belief in the safekeeping power and love of God. Now, she concluded that if she were to die here in this horrible situation that she would still hold fast to her faith. Yet, she could not help but wonder where God was in all of this, it was difficult to see.

"Too awful, too awful," she cried. "It is too much grief to bear. My mind refuses to accept this nightmare as reality."

Deep sobs of desolation came rushing to the surface of her tortured spirit. She moaned in the agony of her despair.

"I am so tired," Shalagh anguished. "Oh, Papa, why, oh why?" she sobbed. "Why did you have to die?"

She tried not to think of the deplorable succession of events that had brought her to this state, but her tortured mind replayed them over and over again.

"One good thing," Shalagh softly mused to herself as she slumped again upon the cold ground, "Mama never had to see her babies taken with fever. Mama was there to greet her two youngest darlings at Heaven's door just a short time after her own parting.

"Sweet babes," Shalagh sighed. "Dark-haired baby Carly, was the picture of Papa and Willy, whose fourth birthday would have been Christmas day, was a cherub with chubby cheeks and golden curls."

"Oh, oh, oh," Shalagh screamed into the swirling snow as memories raced through her mind.

"This pain is too much, I can bear it no longer," she shrieked in agony again and again until finally her voice was gone and would emit no further sound.

No human ear heard her outcry. The sound drifted with the whirling snow wafting away to be recorded eternally with the cries of the earth's oppressed.

"They are now in the presence of Jesus. Safe with Mama and Papa," she whispered with near frozen lips. "They will never cry, be sick or hungry again."

How she longed to be with them at this moment. But, then the sudden thought of her sister brought her back again.

Tara had been so ill with the fever that it was a blessed miracle that she had survived.

"Tara isn't well," mumbled Shalagh. "She needs me and I must return home to be with her."

With great effort she pushed herself to a standing position. She took a step but nearly fell-her strength was gone. She was too cold, hungry and numb to move.

Now above the sound of the wind something caught her attention. At first it was faint and far away-and now closer-yes, there it was again. Now something was coming through the snow. It was coming toward her. Yes Shalagh could dimly make out a figure. A light now came toward her-perhaps it was a delusion of her mind. Oh yes, yes it was a light, a lantern-it could be Caleb and Dylan in search of her.

"Hello," she weakly attempted to shout at the oncoming figure.

There was no answer, still the figure moved toward her.

"Hello," cried Shalagh again.

"Hel-hello," sounded a voice in response to her call.

"Is that you?" Shalagh questioned recognizing the voice that came near her as that of her sister Tara.

In a few seconds they met and clung to each other.

"Oh, Shalagh, dear Shalagh, I was so worried about you," said Tara. "I waited and waited and when you did not come, I had to search for you.

"How did you ever find me?" questioned Shalagh as she staggered and almost fell again.

"God and the angels, I believe," answered Tara. "Come lean on me, we are going home."

"You should not have come out in the storm, Tara, you are too weak," admonished Shalagh. Still she obediently leaned against the comforting arm of her sister to steady herself.

"Take my arm, and we will soon be there," said Tara holding the lantern with her other hand.

Home, thought Shalagh, at least they would be out of the wind but she knew they would have no fuel to build a fire. Unless Caleb and Dylan had been paid for their work that day there would be no food.

Any conversation was difficult above the storm. They struggled on with Shalagh greatly encouraged by the presence of her sister. With heads down they groped against the wind and snow. They leaned on and guided each other. Finally, they passed the stables and barns of Ballymore. They crossed the pasture and staggered through the fields, finally collapsing at the door of the shepherds' cottage.

"Don't stop here!" warned Tara, "you will freeze on the step".

Struggling against the elements Tara pushed open the sturdy door releasing a warm surge of air from within the cottage. She half pulled her near frozen sister into the fire-lit warmth of the room and quickly bolted the door.

"Wha-what is that wonderful aroma?" questioned Shalagh. "An-and a fire-oh it is so warm" as she moved toward the fire, holding out her scraped and icy hands. "Do my senses deceive me?"

Quickly, Tara threw off her cloak and scarf and helped Shalagh remove her wet and partially frozen clothing.

"Sit here, by the fire," said Tara as she covered Shalagh with a warm shawl, "and yes we have food," replied Tara. "Your senses have not deceived you."

Shalagh said nothing as she dropped down gratefully in front of the fire. Tara ladled warm thick soup from a heavy kettle hanging within the hearth into a bowl and carefully placed it into Shalagh's hands.

"Here, take some of this," said Tara bending over Shalagh.

"Whe-Where did you get this from?" marveled Shalagh. "We have had little food for several days.

For a moment, she savored the delicious aroma of the warm brew while holding the bowl close to her face. Then slowly she partook of its mouth-watering contents.

"If this is a dream, let it never end," she smiled wearily.

"Caleb returned from the stables soon after you left this morning." explained Tara. Dylan and he went immediately in search of you. Dylan was positive he could find you but they could not.

"No, I tried a different way," replied Shalagh. "Oh, how I wish they had found me."

"From what Caleb said, if they had succeeded, I suspect they would have taken us with them," declared Tara.

"With them where?" questioned Shalagh.

"They have gone to Derry," answered Tara. "Caleb said if possible they would return sometime tomorrow."

"Thank God," said Shalagh, greatly relieved. "Finally he is going to find Uncle Will and perhaps we can get some help."

"He didn't explain what they were going to do there," declared Tara, "but, it was obvious that he was in great haste. He seemed uneasy and unusually disturbed about something.

"In what way?" petitioned Shalagh.

She knew how upset Caleb was in the months following

Papa's death. He had taken any work he could find trying to provide some means of comfort to the remaining family.

"Well," related Tara as she refilled Shalagh's bowl and brought her a hot cup of tea. "When they could not find you they came back to see if you had arrived home. You had not so they left again, returning in a short time with their arms filled with bags and boxes of food. They left soon, returning again with a large box of peat for the fire. It was at that time that Caleb insisted that upon your return home, we would not leave the cottage. He stated that it was urgent for us to remain inside with the door locked. His face was somber and quite alarming and I sensed he was in fear of something. They left a few minutes later with Papa's gun."

"It would seem they did not travel far to come upon such bounty," reasoned Shalagh as she slowly sipped the tea.

"Perhaps Caleb was given back wages by the overseer," replied Tara with a shrug of her too thin shoulders, " he did not say."

"That is probably what happened," agreed Shalagh, "and it is so dangerous to be out on the road. Why, only yesterday I saw two men fighting over a turnip in the field. It was a good idea to take Papa's gun with them."

"Is there much food?" asked Shalagh as she changed the subject.

"More than I have seen in a long time," answered Tara. "There are turnips, bacon, leeks and cabbage-flour, lard and tea. The cupboard seems quite full."

"Oh, Shalagh, your feet," cried Tara as she looked down in dismay at the appalling rags holding together what was left of her sisters' shoes. "Your feet are cut and bleeding," anguished Tara.

Kneeling down in front of Shalagh she unwound the scraps

of rags from her feet and removed her shoes. Then she brought water from the kettle on the hearth and bathed Shalagh's feet. "I know you care greatly for us," sighed Tara, "but the sharp ground of the fields have cut your shoes to pieces. You will not go out in search of food again."

"I will survive," Shalagh assured her mustering a weak smile, "my feet are as rugged as I am."

"You are just too stubborn to quit," judged Tara, "but no one is invincible, as we well know. Look what happened to poor Papa."

"That may be true," acknowledged Shalagh, "but I am not too unbending to admit that I am tired, so very tired. I think I will just rest a little while," as she curled on the floor by the warm fire.

"Sleep, dear Shalagh," breathed Tara softly as she brought a shawl and placed it around the reposing form of her exhausted sister.

Chapter Three

"Dylan, will you hurry! I am already running behind waiting for you," spoke Cabeb crossly. "Make up your mind, are you coming with me or not."

"I am coming," answered Dylan, "but I am really worried about Shalagh out there alone in search of food."

The two boys left the cottage and started for the stables of Ballymore.

"I think I should have gone with her today," lamented Dylan. "There is nothing to find but still she will not quit.

"I don't care to leave her out there alone either," stated Caleb, "but, the caretaker said he needed help with the horses this morning. Mr. Harcroft told me to bring you along to help and that he would pay us today."

Caleb's collar was pulled high around his face and his head was down away from the cold.

"What did you say?" asked Dylan, as it was difficult to hear above the noise of the wind.

"I said I don't like Shalagh to be out alone searching for food," Caleb replied, "nor do I care to leave Tara alone at the cottage without any fire or food," he continued.

"Do you think that we will really get paid today?" asked Dylan, trying to keep step with his taller brother.

"Well, there is going to be trouble if we don't," declared Caleb assertively.

"How is that?" questioned Dylan.

"From what I hear, which isn't much," said Caleb, "Mr. Harcroft receives money from England to pay the help and-and".

"And what?" yelled Dylan struggling to hear.

"Well, they think he is putting it away for himself," stated Caleb. "He has hardly paid anyone, a piddling here and there, just enough to keep us alive and working."

"What do you think will happen," shouted Dylan.

"There is talk of taking by force what he owes the help," said Caleb. "The help doesn't like me much. They call me the Lord of the Manor and give me the worst jobs. When I think of how good Papa was to his help and how rotten they treat me, well, it just makes me sick. They don't include me in their conversations, only to make fun of me, but I hear them anyway."

"Mr. Harcroft did give you food a few times," stated Dylan, "and these workers were not Papa's."

"Food, I wouldn't call that food. Nothing but scraps off the table left from the days meal," declared Caleb.

"It must be worse for those who don't have a roof over their heads. Shalagh and I see them every day wandering the roads. Some live in the ditches. At least we have shelter," said Dylan.

"You always could see the bright side of a dark day," grumbled Caleb. "If you weren't so dumb, you'd figure out we have no claim to that cottage. When Mr. Harcroft finds out it belongs to the estate, we are out of there. It is only a matter of time."

Dylan hung his head and pulled his collar around his face.

He didn't care to hear anymore and he wasn't fond of being called dumb. He wished that Caleb would treat him with more approval.

The two boys were complete opposites. Caleb at seventeen was tall, blond and brawny. He was an excellent huntsman and horseman, having competed in many riding competitions and had earned a variety of prizes for his efforts. Caleb had also completed one term at the University of Dublin before his father's untimely death. Dylan was only thirteen so his accomplishments were not as remarkable. Until now Dylan had been a happy child who delighted in gently teasing his sisters. They looked upon him with tender affection, while Caleb treated him with superior indifference. In spite of that, Dylan admired Caleb. Dylan favored his dark-haired sisters in appearance. Warm and affectionate of personality he was endowed with a great love for God's creatures and he was forever caring for a hurt or wounded bird or animal. His father and brother's enthusiasm for the hunt brought no joy to Dylan's heart. He was a gifted artist and he loved to sketch the animals he restored to health.

They finished the rest of the three-mile walk to the stables in silence. It was too cold to talk anyway. Dylan had hurried on ahead of Caleb now and reached the stables first.

"Caleb," he yelled back at his brother, "someone must be here. The doors are all standing open."

"No one should be here today but you and me," said Caleb as he hurried toward the barn. "And Mr. Harcroft never comes to the stables this early."

Consisting of several buildings, the stables were spread over a large area. Four of these housed the horses, exquisite thoroughbreds raised by Papa. There was a storage barn for tack and equipment, another held a ring for exercising and show while still another held grain and supplies.

"Where are the horses?" questioned Dylan with a look of unbelief as they entered the first building.

"I don't know, I don't know!" roared Caleb staring at the empty stalls.

Quickly he ran down the length of the long shed.

"They're gone! They're all gone! Where are they?" he yelled. "I'm going to check the other barns, and he ran out the open door at the opposite end.

Dylan caught up with him and followed his brother through the silent empty buildings. There was no one about and everything was gone.

"Even the tack is gone, everything, overnight, all gone, all Papa's horses. I don't believe it," declared Caleb taking off his cap and angrily slapping it against the stone wall. "Someone took them all out in the night. I'll wager you that Mr. Harcroft is gone too, and I'll wager you that he left without paying anyone." He slammed his cap back on top of his head in a state of bewilderment.

"Why would someone do that?" asked Dylan.

"Because," declared Caleb, "this place is too big to run now. The country is in a bad way. They must have shipped the horses off to England, just like they did the dairy herd and everything else. Didn't I tell you that the cottage would be next? They are going to put us out. Tara will never make it with that fever. She needs food and care."

"What are we going to do?" lamented Dylan seeing no bright side at all.

"I'm going up to the house," decided Caleb with renewed determination. "Mr. Harcroft might be there, but I've got a feeling he won't be. Are you coming?"

The boys crossed the fields and pasture and made their way up the frozen hillside to the mansion above. Not too long ago it had been home to them, filled with the love and comfort of family, now it too appeared cold and foreboding. They found the kitchen door wide open and no one about. All of the original help had been dismissed months ago. The housekeeper, who also was the cook, had been brought from England with Mr. Harcroft.

"Mr. Harcroft! Mr. Harcroft!" shouted Caleb as they entered the quiet kitchen. His shouts were greeted by an eerie silence.

A gust of wind from the outside suddenly slammed the kitchen door shut startling both Dylan and Caleb.

"I, I don't think he is here," stuttered Dylan. He was cold hungry and frightened and felt a desperate need to leave.

"I, I th-think we should go," stammered Dylan.

"Don't be such a big baby," admonished Caleb, "look at this mess. Someone certainly made a shambles of this place," continued Caleb as he stepped toward the dining room in search of Mr. Harcroft.

The table and chairs were overturned in the dining room, the bureau drawers were pulled out and the contents strewn everywhere. The parlor was also in disarray with cushions pulled from the chairs and couch, pictures ripped off the walls and furniture overturned.

"What do you think happened?" asked Dylan, wide-eyed in disbelief at what he saw.

"Looks like someone was searching for something," said Caleb as he surveyed the mess.

"You don't suppose they were looking for Mama and Aunt Hala's family jewels?" questioned Dylan.

"Dylan, sometimes I just can't believe you. That is just a stupid story about those old jewels," scoffed Caleb with a disgusted look at Dylan. "There is no truth to it."

"Yes, well Aunt Hala used to tell it for real," Dylan

reminded his brother. "She said great grandmother Boyd had hidden them away when she thought the English were coming. She said that grandmother put a curse on anyone that took them, if they were not a family member."

"Aunt Hala was always making up stories. You know that," said Caleb shaking his head in disgust.

"I know that, but, she said this was a true story and that great grandmother Boyd died without ever telling anyone where she had hidden them," related Dylan.

"Yes, and Aunt Hala told the story often enough that everyone that worked here knew about it," stated Caleb. "I am sure that after all these years that someone would have found them if it were true."

"Come on, let's get out of here before we get blamed for this mess," decided Caleb as he quickly turned toward the door.

Dylan didn't need any coaxing. They scurried through the house and out of the kitchen door and down the hill as fast as they could run toward the cottage.

"We've no choice, Dylan," said Caleb, "we must go to Derry. We have got to try and find Uncle Will and Aunt Hala. Our situation has become too grave. We must seek help or we will die here as our loved ones have before us.

"When will we go?" asked Dylan greatly relieved at what Caleb had said. "We might find help in Derry, but I thought you were angry at Uncle Will and Aunt Hala."

"I am angry," stated Caleb, "but we should have gone a long time ago. Everything just happened so fast, Papa dying, then Mama and the dear babes. Yes, at first I was angry that Aunt Hala and Uncle Will never came to help us. After a while I was so mad I didn't want them to come."

"Why did you change your mind?" questioned Dylan.

"Well, with no job at all, we've got to get away from here.

Besides," the older boy continued, "I've been thinking lately, as close as our families are it is awful strange that we haven't seen or heard from them in all these months. They could be having the same problems we are. Might be they left the country, or worse, they could be dead. We have to go and see," he concluded.

"What if we can't find them?" asked Dylan.

"We'll figure something out," Caleb assured him with a little more tenderness now. We will leave today, as soon as we find Shalagh."

Upon their arrival at the cottage, the boys found that Shalagh had not returned. They left Tara cold and hungry and set out in search of Shalagh. They could find no trace of her anywhere. Finally they gave up after much searching.

"Dylan, come on," declared Caleb, "we are going back to the mansion."

"What for?" asked Dylan.

"That kitchen pantry must be full of food. We are starving and it is apparent that we are not going to receive our wages. If no one is there, we will help ourselves to the food and supplies," answered Caleb.

"Is-Isn't that stealing?" questioned Dylan.

"Everyone is gone. The place is empty. If we don't help ourselves everything will go to waste," explained Caleb.

"I don't know. It doesn't seem right to me," confessed Dylan as he slowly trudged behind his brother as they proceeded back up the hill.

The mansion was the same as when they had left it. No one was there. Quickly, the boys found boxes and containers and filled them with everything they could carry in the way of food.

"Caleb, do you think we ought to go and get the constable?" asked Dylan as they started toward the cottage with their arms loaded down with supplies.

"I just don't trust him," asserted Caleb. "No, I think we should find Uncle Will. We will leave as soon as we get these supplies to Tara."

"Perhaps Shalagh has come back," suggested Dylan. "we can take them with us."

"Let's hope so," replied Caleb. "But Tara is far too weak to travel without the aid of a carriage."

"I fear you are right, Caleb. But perhaps I should stay with them," interjected Dylan. The boy so loved his sisters and felt much closer to them than his older brother.

"I wish you could and I gladly would leave you, but it's a long cold walk to Derry. There's danger all along the way. If something happened to one of us, then it might be that the other could get through for help," explained Caleb.

"You're really scared, aren't you," said Dylan searching his brothers' face.

"You better believe it. We need to get the girls out of Ireland," he answered, "and as fast as we can. There is no safe place here."

"We are leaving Ireland?" gasped Dylan in disbelief.

"It is my hope and prayer," replied Caleb without hesitation.

"Shalagh did not return to the cottage. The boys made two more trips to Ballymore for provisions and still Shalagh did not come home. Finally they could wait no longer.

"We will be back for you tomorrow," promised Caleb to Tara as he built a fire in the fireplace. "You'll be warm and safe here for now. There is plenty of food."

The boys ate in a great hurry and then packed for themselves a small bag of provisions. Night was fast upon them as they hurriedly took to the road for Derry.

"We wasted a good deal of time looking for Shalagh," stated Caleb. "Sure wish we could have left earlier. We'll have to walk all night, now, in the dark and cold."

"Sure you know the way?" inquired Dylan with some reservations.

"Aye, the road takes you straight into Londonderry," Caleb assured him. "We always come this way."

"Do you think we need Papa's gun?" queried Dylan. "It looks awful heavy to carry."

"It just makes good sense to have it with us," stated Caleb as he stopped to check to see if the gun was ready for firing.

Without any warning, Caleb suddenly raised the gun and fired it out across the open snowy field.

"What did you do that for?" screamed Dylan holding his ears and staring at Caleb in total dismay. "You scared me half to death. You think I'm dumb. I think that was dumb. I can't even hear," complained Dylan shaking his head.

"Oh, you will be all right in a minute," declared Caleb. "I wanted to see if it worked. It hasn't been fired since Papa died. You are such an infant Dylan."

Dylan didn't care to discuss it any further. He wanted nothing to do with the gun that had killed Papa, but he wasn't about to argue with Caleb. He would not win anyway.

They were now rounding the hill on which the mansion of Ballymore sat above them.

"Look, Caleb, there is a light in the mansion. Do you suppose that Mr. Harcroft has returned," questioned Dylan.

"So there is a light," observed Caleb peering through the darkness. "Let's take a look."

They climbed the snowy hill with great care and difficulty and then quietly and stealthy made there way to a parlor window.

"The light is coming from the study," whispered Caleb. "Mr. Harcroft must be there. Wait here, I'm going to get the money due me. The front door is wide open anyway.

"Caleb, wait!" cautioned Dylan. "I don't think you should. Let's just go."

"Shhh," silenced Caleb putting his finger to his lips. "Stay here. I'll be right back. That scoundrel is going to pay me."

Caleb entered the spacious front hallway and followed the flickering light which was coming from Papa's study just off the parlor. The parlor and study were joined by wide sliding double doors. They were open, as they had been earlier in the day. Caleb moved quickly across the parlor with its thick plush carpet toward the study door. As he entered the study the dying flames of a great log, glowed red in the fireplace. This was the only light. It had probably burned all day and now the light was visible in the darkness of night.

Caleb turned to leave just as the dying log snapped into with a great crackling sound and sent tiny fingers of blue and gold flame spilling from within. Sparks flew upwards towards the chimney as the fire vainly attempted to rekindle its spent remains. Startled by the noise, Caleb jumped, and at the same time stumbled over something on the floor. It was the mantel clock. He could see it now in the dim unsteady light. It was badly broken. It had been in the family for many years and Caleb had always been fond of its sweet toned punctual chimes. As a small child he had learned to tell time by the precise movement of its hands. Like everything else in his life, the clock lay silent and broken at his feet. He stood his gun against the desk and kneeling he turned the clock toward him. The face glass was shattered. He gave it a gentle shake, hoping it would start, but the chimes only rattled and clanged against each other. In anger and despair, Caleb raised the mantel clock over his head and dashed it to the floor. Now it would never work again. They could have it. They could have it all-Ballymore-everything. Caleb felt he could not go on, but then suddenly.

"Wha-what is this?" he mumbled to himself his hand shaking with excitement.

The mantel clock had fallen apart and jewels came spilling out from somewhere inside the antique clock. Necklaces, rings, broaches all were glistening in the remaining firelight. Caleb reached down and picking them up, let them fall through his fingers. It was then that he saw it, a cold deathly face staring up at him with icy blank eyes from under the desk. The appearance of the corpse was grotesque. There was no doubt about it. It was Mr. Harcroft. His forehead was gashed open with an ugly wound. He was stiff and rigid and had been there for some time.

Caleb scrambled to pick up the jewels. He stuffed his pockets full and felt to see if there were any more.

"Caleb, Caleb! Someone is coming," echoed Dylan's voice from the parlor. Some men are coming on horseback with lanterns. Hurry, Caleb, we must leave."

"All right, I'm coming," yelled Caleb as he gave one more searching glance at the floor while trying to avoid looking in the direction of the desk."

Dylan escaped out the front door just as the constable and two men entered into the kitchen. As Caleb reached the front entrance another of the constable's men met him at the front door.

"Where do you think you're going," demanded the stranger as he held a long gun to Caleb's chest.

Suddenly Caleb was surrounded as bright lanterns glared into his face.

"What are you doing here?" demanded the constable.

"I-I work here," answered Caleb.

"Ya, sure," said one of the men. "You're working in a house that is all torn up with hardly any light?"

"What do you know about all of this," questioned the constable pointing to the overturned furniture.

"I don't know anything about it," replied Caleb. "I came here to get my back wages. The front door was standing open and I saw a light in the study, but, but there wasn't anyone there, just the fire burning in the fireplace."

Immediately, Caleb wished he hadn't mentioned the study. The grim picture of what he had just witnessed turned his face an ashen white. His hands shook and he tried to still them by shoving them into his pockets. He could not do this for his pockets were stuffed with his great grandmother's jewels.

"Check the study!" yelled the constable to one of his men.

Caleb's heart beat rapidly.

"I should have come over here sooner. I got a complaint early this morning about some strange goings on at Ballymore Farm and I guess they were right," said the constable. "Find anything?" he yelled toward the study.

"Same thing as the rest of the house," answered the voice from the study. "Everything is turned upside down and sideways. Wait a minute-wait a minute you'd better get in here."

Caleb felt sick.

"Keep your gun on him," demanded the constable as he quickly entered the study.

"It's the caretaker. He-he's dead," explained the man in the study. "This could be the weapon. Yes, it's been fired recently," added the man as he picked up the gun Caleb had left standing against the desk.

"This your gun boy?" quizzed the constable as he stood between the double-doors that separated the study from the parlor.

"Look over here. There's a cash box open and lying empty on the floor," yelled one of the other men who had followed the constable into the study.

"What did you do with the money, boy?" taunted the constable. "You got something in your pockets? Let's have a look."

Just as the constable started toward Caleb to examine his pockets, a scream of the most terrifying sound rent the air. It came from the direction of the kitchen. Then they heard the sound of breaking and smashing of glass and then another blood curdling scream.

"What the…is that?" roared the constable. "Give me your lantern, Grady."

Grady, one of the men handed his lantern to the constable just as another scream erupted. Its sound was so fearful that for a moment it startled everyone. They seemed frozen in fright. But not Caleb, he mustered his strength and took one flying leap down the hall and out the door. He never stopped to look back as he slipped and slid all the way to the bottom of the hill. He didn't know where to go and had no idea where Dylan had gone. Reaching the road, he tried to run but his breath was leaving him. He covered a short distance along the road before he looked back. He had heard no sound of anyone following him. But, now he could hear horses hoofs pounding fast and hard on the frozen ground. They were coming faster now. It seemed there was no escape. Yes, they were almost upon him now. He wished the earth would open up and hide him. Then swish right beside him. He dared not look up.

"Caleb, Caleb, climb up, take hold," it was Dylan's voice.

"Oh, Dylan," he gasped. "Where did you come from? Where did you get the horse?"

"I stole the constable's horse. Here, you take the reins and I will cling to you," offered Dylan.

With one leap, Caleb swung himself upon the horse and they took off at a rapid pace.

"I chased the rest of the horses away," explained Dylan, "and I smashed windows and screamed like a Banshee in the kitchen. Did you hear me?"

"Did we hear you? That was you, little brother," laughed Caleb.

"Yes it was—did I do good?" asked Dylan as if seeking his brother's approval while clinging fast to his brother's waist.

"You did good little brother. You did real good," praised Caleb.

Dylan felt good. A sense of pride welled up within him, smiling to himself in the darkness of the night.

Chapter Four

The soft light of morning broke over the terrain coloring the eastern sky with varied hues of rose and pale pink. The sun climbed slowly, emerging from behind low lying purple clouds casting bright rays of light over the still countryside.

As it continued to soar higher in the firmament, the vivid sunshine glistened with sparkling brilliance as it danced across the snowy fields. If there was any hope at all left in the hearts of Ireland's people the appearance of the sun brightly shinning for the first time in many days should lift their spirits. Still, however bright it might appear or what promise of warmth it could offer was only superficial.

The suns bright light could not heal the land nor bring food to the hungry or medicine to the sick. Shalagh awoke that morning momentarily unsure of her surroundings. She forced herself to sit up from her crumpled position on the hard floor. Sunshine poured in from the open cottage door.

"Is it morning, Tara?" she questioned putting her hand up to shield the light from her unaccustomed eyes. "I thought I just went to sleep."

"I am sorry," said Tara. "I didn't mean to waken you. The fire was low and when I built it up the room seemed smoky. I opened the door to freshen the air and I guess the light woke you."

"That's all right," said Shalagh with a yawn. She felt stiff and still tired and wrapping the shawl about herself, she sat close to the fire.

"It is so comfortable and warm in here," she mumbled, hugging the shawl still closer about her. "I can't believe that the sun is really shining.

"Yes, it has been up for some time," stated Tara, as she shut the door and bolted it. "In fact it is almost noon."

"Did I really sleep that long," smiled Shalagh, who was usually the first to be up in the morning.

"You were very tired," said Tara as she laid bacon in a pan over the fire to cook.

"Oh Tara, is that really bacon you are preparing?" questioned Shalagh.

"It is and I waited for you to awake so we could eat together," explained Tara. "You will not go out any longer in search of food. We have plenty for now."

"Caleb and Dylan have not returned?" asked Shalagh.

"Not as yet, but I am sure they will come soon," answered Tara.

"I hope and pray they are safe and that they are able to bring Uncle Will back with them," Shalagh sighed.

"Perhaps Aunt Hala will also come and take us back to Londonderry with them," suggested Tara.

Shalagh arose and helped Tara prepare the noon meal. The bacon snapped and sizzled as the pleasant aroma filled the dim smoky room. They worked together in eager anticipation of the joy of eating. Shalagh quickly made biscuits while Tara stirred a hot porridge in a kettle hanging over the open fire. Finally, they sat down and said their morning prayers thanking God for the meal they were about to partake of. They ate in silence, savoring every bite. As they finished eating Tara sat sadly picking crumbs from her lap and placing them in her mouth.

"I miss Momma and Poppa something awful," she said with tears welling up in her eyes.

"We all do Tara," comforted Shalagh, but they are gone and we must make the best of it. We will always have happy memories of them and someday we will see them again. That is a promise from God's Word."

"I know, but I just wish I could have Momma knock on our bedroom door and call us down to breakfast one more time," reminisced Tara as she stared wistfully into space."

The two sisters continued on for some time relating happy times they had shared at Balleymore. Later they straightened and tidied the cottage as much as was possible in spite of the dirt floor and smoke covered walls. Neither left the cottage for any length of time as Caleb had requested. Then just as they were about to warm the evening meal, Shalagh thought she heard something.

"Listen," she said putting her finger to her lips, "I think someone is coming up the path to the cottage."

"She hurried to the door in anticipation that it would be Caleb and Dylan as Tara followed her close behind. Before they could open the door, someone pounded loudly on the other side. Shalagh quickly pulled open the door to face none other than the constable of law who was accompanied by two deputies. They recognized both of them as having worked for their father at one time.

"Shalagh Frizzle?" questioned the officer.

"Yes," she replied hesitantly, knowing full well the constable had known her family forever.

"I have a writ here that states that all tenants must vacate the premises of this property immediately," he declared waving a piece of paper for her to see.

"I...I don't understand," stammered Shalagh, her throat suddenly gone dry.

"This document states," and he now held it up as though he were reading it, "that any person or persons abiding anywhere on this estate must leave today. The land is to be cleared of all occupants by authority of the Crown."

"You—you mean now?" gasped Tara, "tonight?"

"That is correct," he acknowledged with an affirmative nod of his head.

"Oh, you can't enforce such a law against us," cried Shalagh, "we have no place to go."

"I must carry out my orders," he disclosed. "This cottage is to be torn down tonight," he finished turning his head nervously away to avoid Shalagh's tearfully searching eyes.

"Michael Shay, you know as well as I do that it was our own dear father who saved your family from the brink of starvation. It was he who got you this very job. Can you show us no mercy?" pleaded Shalagh. "And you Orin Moran," Shalagh continued turning to one of the men, "how is the little one who was so ill? She must be going on five or so I would think. Near death she was too. She would have died had Papa not brought in a doctor all the way from Belfast and paid for her doctoring it comes to my mind."

"We cannot help any of that now," stated the constable, "we must do our duty and enforce our orders. Someone did away with the caretaker at the Manor House. They ransacked the place and took all the valuables. The man was murdered in cold blood."

"Oh, we did not know," moaned Shalagh drawing back as fear gripped her heart with long icy fingers.

"What have we to do with it all?" questioned Tara now stepping forward. "We did not murder or rob the man."

"I would not be too sure of that," retorted the officer with a sneer on his face. "Your brother Caleb is our prime suspect. We know he isn't here but the contents of this house may make you girls a party to murder."

"Search the cottage men," he commanded and then tear it down.

Instantly Shalagh came alive as fire shot from the depths of her deep blue eyes.

"You will not touch a thing in this place until we have removed our belongings, little that we have," Shalagh screamed. "Then you can tear it down, burn it, whatever you wish, I don't care. But I warn you, if you cross this threshold before we remove our possessions your souls will burn in hell. The devil himself will come to get you with a horde of demons. I promise it will happen."

Constable Shay wasn't known to be a religious man, but he was superstitious. He knew the background of this devout God fearing family. He backed off fearing Shalagh may have enough sway with God to have such a punishment delivered upon him.

"All right then," he grumbled with an inward shudder. "I'll give you time to pack your things and be out of here."

The two girls made haste, massing every bit of food they could into the bags their brothers had brought them in. They threw what turf they could carry into a basket. Erratically they chose of what was left of their family's possessions. As they passed through the door, the order was given to push down the walls.

"You will pay for this," rebuffed Shalagh as she and Tara, bent under their heavy loads, walked close by Michael Shay. "My brother never hurt anyone and you know it. If God doesn't punish you the Devil will and that is a promise," assured Shalagh.

"Go on with you," he grunted, "before I change my mind and put you both in the work house."

"Come Shalagh," anguished Tara. "Leave him be, there is nothing more we can do. Let us put as much space between us and these awful men as we can."

"Mercy, I hope they do not decide to come after us," gasped Shalagh as they struggled along the road with their heavy and cumbersome bags.

"Where will we go?" asked Tara, not sure of their destination. "We cannot go far carrying these heavy loads."

"I don't know," answered Shalagh, "that is I am not sure. Well, I guess we will go to Derry. We must find Caleb and Dylan."

"To Derry?" gasped Tara, "we will not be able to walk five miles down the road like this. We could never walk to Derry and it…it will soon be dark."

They struggled on in silence. Glancing back they could see smoke rising from the area that had been their only means of shelter. Darkness descended and the bitter cold became more acute. The pain in Shalagh's feet was intense. Tara, who had remained fairly calm until now, yielded suddenly to despair.

"We are not going to make it, Shalagh," she cried. "We could never walk all the way to Londonderry in this cold. Look at your shoes, they are tattered rags. Even if we did get there what good would it do us? We don't know how to find Caleb and Dylan. We may as well die here."

She began to hurry ahead now, dropping things all along the way. Just down the road was the little cemetery where the family lay buried and it was to this place she ran. She threw open the creaky rusty gate at the entrance and plunged headlong, throwing her self upon her mother's grave. She was completely overcome with grief and fatigue and cried with deep uncontrolled sobs.

"I will die here," she proclaimed with final resolution. "I

will lie here until death overtakes me and I join our loved ones above."

Shalagh had followed closely behind her, attempting to pick up what she could carry of Tara's discarded belongings. Entering the churchyard Shalagh dropped down on the cold ground near Tara. Now under a heavy weight of despair herself she could not but agree with Tara's decision. She felt too drained of strength to fight anymore.

"Yes, why not give up?" she questioned softly. "No one cares about us." Yes, that is what she too would do. They would just remain here until their spirits' left their bodies and angels would come and transport them to their eternal home. She half glanced at Tara lying prostrate across their mother's grave weeping uncontrollably. Consumed with fatigue and cold, Shalagh allowed herself to collapse upon the frozen ground.

Sometime later, Shalagh awoke with a start. Shalagh had no idea how long she and Tara had been in the cold Cemetery. Slowly she opened her eyes and realized that night had come and it was very dark.

"What...what is that? Who...who are you?" questioned Shalagh as she made an attempt to arise. Then with vain effort she tried to shield her eyes from the sudden appearance of a brilliant light, which appeared unnaturally all around her. It radiated with such luster that she could not see beyond its perimeter. Then a voice spoke from where she did not know. It shook the earth beneath her as it thundered her name.

"Shalagh! Shalagh!" the sound pulsated throughout the atmosphere. "Shalagh," again the voice penetrated through the flowing brightness of dazzling light. A sense of well being—a blissful and joyful warmth embraced Shalagh's near frozen body.

Shalagh looked at Tara for some response, but the younger

girl never moved. Tara lay undisturbed by the lyric voice that chimed through the still night air of the churchyard. A sense of euphoric well being and joy engulfed Shalagh as a Holy peace fell upon her. The cold ground beneath her became warm and the warmth flowed through her body. She was lifted by an unseen force, which caused her to stand painlessly upon her cut and bruised feet. Suddenly, before her eyes stood an angelic being huge in statue and of unstained, uncorrupted divine perfection. Shalagh tried to draw back but she could not move. Its' beauty was beyond anything she could ever imagine. She squinted, shielding her eyes again to see more clearly through the radiating brightness of the light all about them.

"Ha...Have you come to take us home to heaven?" stammered Shalagh. She trembled not so much in fear but in awe. She was ready to go, desired to go, but still she shook uncontrollably.

"It is not your time to come," spoke the heavenly messenger as the sound of his voice reverberated and shook the earth again. "You have much work to do. Look onward over and across the fields to the west toward the horizon," said the angel while pointing with one long finger of his hand.

Shalagh stared in the direction suggested, but saw only the dark snow covered graveyard.

"Look! Look!" spoke the thundering voice again now filled with urgent anticipation.

"I am looking, but I see only the cold ground and barren trees," answered Shalagh in a weak quivering voice. "What do you want me to see?"

"Look now!" spoke the figure.

In trusting obedience Shalagh strained her eyes peering into the dark, yes there was something there. She could see it now. Yes, beyond the dark folds of night...

"Oh my, Oh my," gasped Shalagh in astonishment.

Before her now she beheld a beautiful river of azure blue as the air turned warm all around her. Bright sunshine danced across the rippling water. On one side of the wide, fast flowing river were tall trees of various kinds. The leaves were ornamented with colors of red and gold and brown. On the opposite side were orchards with branches of ripe fruit so heavy they touched the ground. Cattle grazed peacefully among the trees. White seagulls circled in the air above. Shalagh listened intently as she heard the sound of children's voices happy at play. She did not see or clearly understand them but knew they were close by. Swans swam contentedly in the rushes along the shore. She stood in amazement for some moments. Then so overcome by the reality of the scene she reached out her hand to touch the deliciously appearing fruit so near her, in an instant it was gone. Shalagh turned to face the messenger believing she had witnessed a scene from heaven.

"Ha...have I looked into heaven?" Shalagh questioned.

Ignoring her question the figure asked a question in return. "Have you not been taught to think on these words? What I tell you now in darkness, shout abroad when daybreak comes. What I whisper in your ear shout from the housetops for all to hear."

"Yes, yes I will try," proclaimed Shalagh, "but there is little I can do if I die here."

"The sparrows of the air do not fall to the ground unnoticed. Fear not, you are of more value than many sparrows," replied the angelic figure.

"Awake your sister," commanded the angel pointing to Tara. "Leave this place. Go quickly to the nearest city. Wake her now. Do not delay.

As fast as it had appeared the brilliant light became

prismatic and the radiance began to fade. The light and figure vanished. Shalagh was left behind in the empty cold darkness all about her. She trembled in fearful reverence of what she had just seen. Then upon the cold ground she bowed to her knees and worshipped her Lord. When finished she stood with a new assurance, sure of her redemption through the blood of Jesus Christ and positive of God's protective power and deliverance. In that dark graveyard, caught in the grip of death's heinous claws Shalagh believed that El Shaddai was able and more than enough. Now she took a step toward Tara and then another step. There was no pain. She was walking without pain in her feet. She reached down and felt of her shoes. They were still tattered and held together with rags, but there was no pain.

"Tara, Tara, wake up," she shouted reaching down to touch her sister.

Tara lay cold and lifeless upon the ground.

"Oh, Tara, Tara, please get up," pleaded Shalagh. "Father, please help me."

There was no response from Tara.

"Tara, Tara, get up! Get up now! We have to leave," Shalagh begged.

Still there was no reply, no movement, nothing but the sighing of the wind. Now Shalagh demanded that Tara awake.

"You will not lie here and die. I will not let you," wept Shalagh as she forcibly took hold of and shook Tara's limp body in a desperate attempt to restore life into it. Realizing she could not wake her, Shalagh allowed Tara's body to slump back against the ground and then in a soft and gentler tone, Shalagh spoke again.

"Taryn Margot Frizzle," she said taking her sister's icy hand in hers, "In the name of Jesus Christ, who is the resurrection and the life, rise Tara, rise."

Shalagh felt a response, a movement. Tara's hand began to warm.

"Wha…what are you doing," sputtered Tara. "Why—why are you shaking me?"

"Oh, Tara," cried Shalagh with great relief, you have slept long enough. Come dear sister, we must go."

"But I am tired," moaned Tara.

"It is not time to sleep. Come we must go," enforced Shalagh while pulling Tara up to stand upon her own feet. Then she led Tara through the bleak cemetery, out through the gate and onto the road beyond.

"Wait here, I will be back in a minute," Shalagh implored.

Returning to the graveyard she picked up the provisions she had dropped and carried them back to where Tara stood waiting.

"Tara, we must go now and I need you to help me carry these things," said Shalagh.

"What has come over you?" groaned Tara with a shiver. "It is too dark and cold to travel tonight."

"It is important that we go now," said Shalagh. "I will explain it all later. Right now let us pick up as much as we can carry and try to reach Londonderry."

Shalagh spoke with such command in her voice that Tara reached down and picked up her share of the load and followed her sister who was already moving down the snow covered road.

The snow had stopped momentarily and a pale wanton moon appeared high in the spectral sky. Somewhere across the moors a dog howled a mournful cry. Then after they had traveled some distance down the road they stopped startled by a distant sound echoing across the fields.

"What is that?" questioned Tara looking back.

"I don't know," answered Shalagh inquisitively as she too looked back but saw nothing. After a moment of silence Shalagh said, "Let's move on, I don't hear it now."

"There, there it is again," offered Tara stopping to look back as the sound wafted toward them and drifted away again.

Whatever it was had a bell-like metallic sound.

"Oh...I see something moving towards us along the road," cringed Tara staring hard into the distance at an oncoming object. "What is it?" she questioned.

"I do not know," stated Shalagh. "It is too far away to tell, but it seems that the air rings with the sound of bells."

"Oh, what if it is the constable and his men," whimpered Tara. "They will put us in the workhouse or worse prison. What shall we do?"

"I do not think it is them," retorted Shalagh, "but if it is we will hide in the ditch by the side of the road."

The specter was now closing the distance between them at a fast rate of speed.

"Tara, I...I can see it now," explained Shalagh.

"Yes, then what is it Shalagh," asked Tara now too afraid to look back.

"It., it is a horse, yes a horse and I think a sleigh," said Shalagh staring hard attempting to more clearly see the object in the distance.

"A sleigh?" gasped Tara. "Do you think the constable would pursue us in a sleigh?"

In a matter of minutes the horse and sleigh was upon them. The lone occupant, the driver, witnessed the two girls standing by the side of the road gripping their heavy bundles.

"Whoa there Prince," he called bringing the sleigh to a sudden halt in front of them.

The horse was enormous and a sight to behold as it pawed

the ground and snorted impatiently rearing to go. Dozens of spherical bells fixed to the harness straps and all around the frame of the sleigh glistened in the dim moonlight and jingled at every movement of the horse and sleigh.

"What is it my lassies," the driver shouted down to them from the seat in front of the sleigh.

He took a lighted lantern from its post by the seat and held it high to better see them. He was dressed in furs even to his hat, which partially covered his head of snow-white hair.

Shalagh squinted and stared. There was something about that face that seemed to resemble the angelic being she saw in the graveyard. Her mouth fell open as she intently pondered his features.

"You'd be thinking I was a spirit or something by the look on your lovely faces," said the driver. And thus said he laughed a hearty laugh throwing his head back causing the horse to jump and shake the bells into lyrical ringing.

"Where would you be going at this time of the night and in the cold?" he questioned in a good-natured tone of voice.

"We are on our way to Londonderry," replied Shalagh while regaining some composure.

"Well you have a long walk ahead of you," he stated. "Would you be liking a ride my fine ladies? I am taking the mayor of Londonderry's fine sleigh and horse to his grace from the stables some miles south of here. It's safer to travel at night, so I thought I would get the job done. The whole back seat is empty so throw you bags up to me and climb aboard. It's much better than walking," he assured them with a smile.

Hardly able to believe their good fortune, Shalagh and Tara handed up their things to the driver who quickly deposited them underneath the front seat. Climbing into the sleigh the girls found thick fur blankets on the seat for use as covers. They crawled between the blankets pulling them close around them. Without another word from the driver the sleigh suddenly lurched forward and flew down the snow covered road in the direction of Derry.

"Perhaps he is an angel in disguise," laughed Tara in jest as she snuggled close to Shalagh.

"And well he might be," agreed Shalagh completely serious. "Well he might be."

Chapter Five

The large sleigh was well lighted with lanterns in front and back. The horse and driver had no difficulty maneuvering the sled successfully over the frozen snow. They appeared to move smoothly and without effort. Soon snow began to fall again but it was of little matter at the moment. Wrapped snuggled in warm fur blankets in the temporary safety of their fast moving transportation, Tara fell soundly asleep. Shalagh was equally weary, but her thoughts would not allow her to rest. She was enthralled by what she had experienced in the silent confines of the churchyard. She marveled at God's divine intervention. El Shaddai had guided them unto the road at the perfect time to meet the sleigh. Positive she and Tara were under God's protection, Shalagh now asked for wisdom.

"Please help us to find Aunt Hala and Uncle Will," she prayed aloud, "and unite us with our dear brothers.

Silently, she prayed for some time. Then her thoughts wandered as to where Caleb and Dylan could be. Perhaps they had found Uncle Will and returned to the cottage finding it in dismal ruins. Somehow, she sensed that was not true. If Caleb knew the constable was looking for him for the murder of the caretaker, he would not dare to return to Ballymore. The law could be searching for him even in Derry. He would have to be very careful.

Tara's head nodded against Shalagh's shoulder.

"I'm glad she can sleep," thought Shalagh. "She is going to need all the rest she can get for what may lay ahead of us."

Shalagh attempted to map out a plan. As soon as they arrived in Londonderry, She and Tara would find Aunt and Uncles house. She was sure it would be easy to find. It was still a mystery why Aunt and Uncle had not come to their aid. Aunt Hala and Mama were always there for each other—holidays, birthdays, celebrations and sickness—sometimes and most often for no reason at all. The two sisters often shopped together in Derry, stopping to have lunch with Uncle Will at the mill. How could it be, that when Mama needed her most Aunt Hala did not come to her aid. The absence of Aunt Hala and Uncle Will had truly been incomprehensible. However, the severity of the ensuing struggle to survive left no intimate moments in which to justify or seek out a reason for their unnatural absence.

Shalagh held in her heart forever keepsakes of happy memories regarding Aunt Hala. Unable to have children of her own until some years after her younger sister Taryn, Aunt Hala had been a second mother to Shalagh and her siblings. In fact, Shalagh was her aunt's namesake. As a small child, Mama could not pronounce her older sister's name and thus shortened it to Hala. The name remained as such throughout the ensuing years.

A smile crossed Shalagh's face as she recalled with fondness, Aunt Hala's talent for putting stories to song. With her sweet melodious voice she would act them out in operatic form. Sometimes the theater would be the orchard filled with the fragrant blossoms of spring. The children would clap their hands with delight as Aunt Hala sang and danced amidst the falling petals gently floating down to a carpet of green grass under the trees. Other times this sprightly lady would put on a play or a skit in the huge parlor or study of Ballymore with the fire snapping merrily on the hearth. Mama had often joined her audacious sister in the dramatic display of artistry as the children watched with great admiration and appreciation.

Time slipped away and became of little importance to Shalagh as she was so engrossed in her thoughts and memories. When she finally became aware of her surroundings, they were well within the city wall of Derry.

Suddenly the sleigh gave a lurch to one side and came to an abrupt stop. Tara awoke startled by the sudden jolt. The driver pulled the sleigh up to the side of a long low building.

"This is as far as I can take you ladies," shouted the driver, "unless you've business in the Thornehill District. That is where the mayor lives and my destination.

"Thornehill?" questioned Shalagh. "Perhaps you might know the Frizzle family of Thornehill District, the Will Frizzle family," she added.

"No ma'm, I don't," he kindly explained. "I spend most of my time on the farm in lower Derry. I don't know many people in Thornehill. If you've no place to spend the night I suggest you go around to the back door of this building. The good Quakers will help you," he informed them. He took a step down from the sleigh and began to transfer the girls' belongings from under the front seat to the snowy ground.

The girls gingerly stepped down as the driver put the last of their possessions on the ground. He stared at them for a second, then reached up and took down two of the fur robes and handed them to the ill-clad girls. Then he quickly bounded back upon the sleigh and was gone before they could thank him.

"Well, I guess we had better try the back door," suggested Shalagh with a shrug.

They gathered up their belongings and walked around to the other side of the building.

"These blankets are wonderful," said Tara brushing her cheek against the soft fur of the robe, "they will really keep out the cold."

"Yes, they will be a great help," acknowledged Shalagh. "What a kind thing for him to do."

They approached the door in the back of the building and knocked loudly upon it. The results of their rapping soon brought a response. The door was opened by a woman who carried a lighted candle in a holder. She was dressed in the garments of a Quaker. Both girls were ignorant as to the pursuits or endeavors of the Quakers.

"Are you in need of a place to sleep?" questioned the woman in a hushed tone. The expression on her face was sympathetic.

"Yes," spoke the girls together while nodding their heads in agreement.

"Come in then," she said. "You must sign the journal on the table."

"Does everyone sign the journal when they stay here?" questioned Shalagh, thinking Caleb and Dylan may have done so.

"Yes," answered the woman, "we attempt to have everyone sign the register. Are you looking for someone?" she questioned.

"We have come in search of our brothers," stated Shalagh.

"Oh, they would not be here," whispered the lady, "they would be up the hill in the men's and boy's complex.

"I see," nodded Shalagh with evident disappointment in her voice.

"You could go their tomorrow," informed the woman. "I am sure they will try to help you."

After signing their names, they were informed that there were a few cots left in the far corner of the dimly lit room.

"Keep your belongings closely beside you," cautioned the woman noting the assortment of things the girls carried with them. "One more thing," she added, "you must leave when the bell rings at seven in the morning."

It was apparent that the dimly lit room had originally been a warehouse or storage area. It was now occupied by many cots, upon which people were sleeping. A strong unpleasant odor filled the musty air. A lantern hung high on each of the four walls casting eerie flickering shadows over the sleeping forms. The girls carried their heavy belongings through the maze of cots to the far end of the room. Finding only one cot available, Shalagh spread her fur robe on the bare floor leaving the cot for Tara.

This will make it much easier for me to keep watch over our belongings," she explained brushing off any argument whispered by Tara.

Sleep did not come easy for either of the girls. The dawning of morning was not greeted by much joy. The sound of people, some coughing and others moaning and the whimpering cries of the children had not contributed to a good nights rest. It seemed they had just drifted off when the noise of the morning bell and people stirring about woke them.

"Now, I could sleep," lamented Shalagh as she stood up and folded her robe.

"I know," sympathized Tara, who felt weak and feverish, but she did not wish to alarm Shalagh.

As was their usual custom, the girls took out the family Bible and read from it and then bowed their head and prayed.

They asked for wisdom and deliverance in the midst of the clamor made by the homeless who were gathering up their meager belongings. The room was filled with half-starved and poorly clad women and children.

"Poor little waifs," Tara sighed as she despaired for the children. "If only we could help them in some way."

"I know," agreed Shalagh. "My heart breaks at the sight, but there appears to be no solution for the problem."

They gathered up their own things and followed the line of homeless women out the door. Having no idea where to go and having much to carry, they followed the crowd, which led them to a line being formed at a makeshift kitchen. The kitchen was set up in a vacant storefront. The food was passed to the hungry line of eagerly awaiting people through the upper half of an open split door. Each person was given a piece of dried bread and a ladle of watery soup. They had to provide their own containers. Tara and Shalagh took only the bread, having no vessels for the soup.

"You're smart not to drink that swill," said a young woman with a kindly looking face. She was standing in the line behind them. "The bread is safe enough, but the broth could make you sick," she added softly.

"It looks dreadful," agreed Tara making a face at the thought of the disgusting brew, "and it smells even worse," she added

"I know," replied the woman, "the Quakers do the best they can with what little they have to work with. If it were not for their charity, many more would starve. Are you going to the square?" asked the woman.

"I…I don't know," replied Shalagh uncertain as to what the woman meant.

"I did't think to be seeing you girls around here before," said the lady. "My name is Molly Rynn. You're new to the group,

61

aren't you? You've probably not been to the square then," she smiled.

"We only arrived in Derry last night," explained Tara. "We have come in search of our family."

"Yes," added Shalagh. "We are trying to find our brothers."

"Your brothers are here in Derry?" questioned Molly as she took a purse from under her coat and placed the bread she had just been given into the purse.

"We believe they are with our aunt and uncle at their home here in Derry," said Shalagh. "We hope to find our way there today."

"I see," replied Molly. Then you won't be needing to go to the square. Most of these folks will take their food and go there. They've no place else to go. They huddle together and try to keep a big fire going with anything they can find to burn."

"Oh, Molly!" screamed Tara as Molly was suddenly thrown to the ground by two urchin boys who seemed to come from nowhere. One of the ruffians grabbed Molly's purse and started to run. Tara, acting quickly, reached out her foot and tripped the boy, sending him sprawling. As he hit the ground, Shalagh grabbed the purse, pulling it to safety. The boys were gone before the bag could be handed to Molly.

"Oh, Thank you, thank you," repeated Molly gratefully, "thank you so much. I could never repay you girls. I try to be so careful, but I was momentarily careless, just plain careless, it seems."

"We are happy we could help," said Shalagh. "What terrible hooligans and thieves."

"No, they are just desperate children," affirmed Molly, "it was my fault. I always keep the purse under my coat, but I was slow putting the bread away. It's for my boy."

A young lad suddenly appeared before them and interrupting Molly said.

"What happened, Ma?" questioned the boy who was obviously upset.

"Oh, a couple of rowdy lads tried to steal my purse," Molly explained, "but these young ladies got it back for me. I am fine," she assured the boy as she brushed herself off and checked her purse.

"Where'd they go? I'll get 'em," said the boy, anger flaring in his dark eyes.

"No, they are long gone," replied Molly with a flick of her hand adding, "let it be."

"Girls, this is my son, Danny," said Molly with a look of pride.

The boy appeared to be about the age of Dylan. He was dark complexioned with black curly hair. Now he graciously shook hands with Tara and Shalagh as they both introduced themselves.

"My other boy is down on the dock and I was saving food for him," explained Molly. "I sure wish I could repay you girls in some way."

"Well, you could tell us how to find the sleeping quarters for the men," stated Shalagh. "We need to know if our brothers have been there."

"Sure, Danny and I will take you there. It is just up the hill," smiled Molly, obliged to help the girls in any way she could.

"If we do not find them we will go to our aunt and uncles house in Thornehill," explained Shalagh.

"Thornehill?" That's clear on the other side of town. Real nice part of town, I might add. Is that where your relatives live?" she questioned noting the girls ragged appearance.

"Yes, at least we hope they still live there," answered Shalagh optimistically.

"How are you going to get there?" asked Molly.

"I guess we will walk," stated Shalagh.

"It's going to be awful hard to walk and carry all your belongings with you uphill and down," surveyed Molly looking in that direction. "You've got a lot to carry. Why don't you leave your things with me and my boys. We've got a place where we could keep them safe for you. It isn't smart to have those fur robes out for people to see. They'll kill to get them."

"Oh, I don't know," Shalagh hesitated looking at Tara.

Tara shrugging her shoulders and surveying all their belongings questioned, "How can we carry all these things with us?"

"I guess we can't," Shalagh sighed resolutely. "Well, if you don't mind."

"Then it's settled," concluded Molly. "The boys and I will meet you right here in this same place tonight when we come for food."

The decision was made and the girls left their belongings with Molly. Danny then accompanied them to the Quaker men's quarters with great hope that Caleb and Dylan had been there. No one by that name had registered there. Disappointed they left Danny behind and began the long walk to Thornehill.

Chapter Six

With unrelenting determination Shalagh and Tara pressed on ever hopeful of finding Aunt Hala and Uncle Wills' residence. Previously they had always traveled in the company of adults and this was their first attempt to find their aunt and uncle on their own.

"It can't be that hard to find," lamented Shalagh after they had unsuccessfully tried street after street and had climbed one hill after another. Still they were unable to recognize any familiar territory.

"We should have brought one of the fur blankets with us to keep warm," expressed Tara, "and do we have anything to eat? I am very hungry."

"I have some pieces of bread in my pocket," soothed Shalagh. We will rest here by this building for a moment.

Shalagh removed some dried bread crusts from the inner pocket of her clothing and shared them with Tara. They huddled beside the column of a large building to shield themselves from the raw biting wind.

"You have been walking with such strength," declared Tara, "your feet must not pain you so much today."

There was momentary silence broken by Shalagh's softly spoken response, "I have no pain in them at all."

"Oh, Shalagh, perhaps they are frost bitten. You feel no pain at all?" questioned Tara with a look of concern.

"I...I...I had a most unusual experience in the graveyard last night while you were asleep. It would be difficult for anyone to understand if they had not witnessed what I saw," explained Shalagh. "An angel of the Lord appeared and touched my feet and made them completely whole."

Now silence fell upon Tara as she stared at Shalagh with an inquisitive look of unbelief.

"You...you are teasing me, aren't you?" grinned Tara with an incredulous glance at her sister.

"I am not teasing you Tara," replied Shalagh with a serious tone to her voice. "It really happened. An angel came to the cemetery. He told me to wake you and for us to leave quickly and go to the nearest city."

"You are not joking are you?" demanded Tara. "You really did see an angel?"

"Yes, and I heard his voice and I will never, never forget it," stated Shalagh. "Not only did he speak, but he showed me a warm place with a beautiful river flowing through it. There were luscious fruit trees laden heavy with delicious fruit along the rivers' shoreline. Cattle grazed peacefully on green grass along the river banks and..."

"Oh! Shalagh—Shalagh! I dreamed of such a place as you describe. Yes, yes as I slept there in the cemetery. It was so beautiful that I did not want to leave. I believed it was Heaven. I thought you would be upset if I told you," related Tara.

"How strange," thoughtfully mused Shalagh. "I mean that I would see such a place and that you would dream of it at the same time."

"Do you think we saw into Heaven?" asked Tara. "I didn't see Mama, Papa or the dear babes though. Did you see them Shalagh?"

"No, I did not see them either. But wouldn't it be wonderful to be in that warm, lovely country right now, picking fruit from the trees," shivered Shalagh. "I guess we had better hurry on. It is getting late."

They started on their way again still reflecting on their recent conversation.

"I was afraid you would not understand if I told you about last night," said Shalagh.

"I must admit, I really don't," stated Tara, "however, I am happy for you."

"For both of us," said Shalagh, "had the angel not woke us we would have died there. I truly believe he saved our lives."

The walk now went more rapidly with Shalagh relating and sharing the glorious events that had taken place the night before. Tara was greatly touched by what Shalagh had told her.

After much time, they finally arrived at the stately home of their aunt and uncle. As they made their way up the walk to the verandah, they could not help but reminisce silently of the wonderful happy times they had shared here with family.

After several applications upon the door-knocker a butler in full uniform appeared. He scanned their apparel with a look of disgust.

"Be off with you," he sneered. "You've no business here. We don't allow beggars, not even at the back gates."

He stepped forward motioning with his gloved hands for them to depart.

"But...but, sir," cried Tara! We have come to see our Aunt, Mrs. Will Frizzle." She darted swiftly past the flailing hands of the butler.

"Aunt Hala," she called while bursting through the open door.

She stepped into the now familiar hallway and would have

continued, but was stopped abruptly by the butler who grabbed her by the back of her coat collar. He lifted her off her feet and threw her flying through the air. She landed on her hands and knees a few feet from the verandah.

"Oh, you monster!" screamed Shalagh, running to the aid of her sister. "How could you be so cruel and so uncaring. We only wanted to speak to our aunt and uncle."

Shalagh reached Tara and helped her up from her disheveled position on the ground. Tara's skirt was torn and her knees badly scraped. The butler turned and strode back into the house slamming the door behind him.

"Oh, poor Tara," soothed Shalagh. "That was an awful thing that he did to you. You should never, never be treated like that."

"I am not hurt, not really," insisted Tara brushing the snow from her clothing. "It did shake me up a bit, but I am all in one piece. What will we do now?" she asked looking at Shalagh for direction.

"We could try going around to the back," suggested Shalagh, "perhaps the help would let us in."

"What if he is watching us?" questioned Tara. "I don't want to meet up with him again."

"We will have to be careful," Shalagh cautioned her. "Let us go out to the front walk and around the block to the back of the house."

After some maneuvering they finally arrived at the kitchen situated in the back of the house. They rapped on the door and a maid in uniform soon appeared.

"No," she assured them, no one lived there by the name of Frizzle. She explained that she had been in the household only a few weeks and knew nothing of the former owners. With that she shut the door and left them standing alone in the cold.

"Whatever are we going to do?" groaned Tara hugging her arms about her frail body trying to keep out the cold.

"I guess it would be best if we go back to Molly and retrieve our belongings," said Shalagh. "It is getting late and it will be dark soon. Come," she continued in exasperation. "They are not here." Huddled together they started down the street for the long walk back. They hadn't gone too far when Tara stopped and looked behind them.

"Is that woman calling us?" she questioned.

Sure enough a woman, also dressed in a maid's uniform with a dark shawl thrown over her shoulders came scuttling toward them.

"Wait up! Wait up!" she called as she closed the distance between them.

"Did I hear you inquiring about the Frizzle family?" she puffed breathlessly as she caught up with them. She drew quick, short breaths of air in and out of her pouchy cheeks.

"Do you know where they are?" quizzed Shalagh as she regarded the nervous appearing woman.

"Well, I tell you it is hard to say," she answered anxiously glancing back over her shoulder with an uneasy look.

"What do you know about them?" questioned Tara with a sound of urgency in her voice.

"Well, I—I know for certain, that the mister is dead," she whispered. "He was killed in an accident at the mill some months ago."

"Oh, it can't be true," sobbed Tara. "Not dear Uncle Will. Please...please tell me it isn't true."

"Oh, my, I shouldn't be here," declared the maid startled by Tara's sudden reaction.

"Aunt Hala and the children?" gasped Shalagh attempting some composure not wanting to frighten the woman away. "What has become of them?"

"I shouldn't be telling you none of this, but I remember you girls and your family. Served you myself right in the dining room. Hardly knew you when I saw you today. But,. I remembered you and I was fond of your aunt and uncle," stated the woman.

"What happened to them?" asked Shalagh.

"Well, it wasn't only a few days after they laid Mr. Will to rest," explained the maid, "that the banks foreclosed on your dear aunt and they took her and the children away."

"Away? Where did they take them?" questioned Tara as she continued to sob.

"I don't know, I'm not sure…debtor's prison or the work house. Word came back that the Mrs. died there—poor dear soul," she sniffled.

"How long ago did this happen?" questioned Shalagh while wiping the tears flowing freely down her cheeks.

"End of summer or early last fall," responded the woman. "The house was sold shortly after that."

"Have you seen our brothers at all?" asked Tara. "Have they been to the house? Do you remember them?"

"I remember them, but, no they have not been to the house at any time that I was there," she assured them.

"Do you know where the work house might be?" asked Shalagh.

"Sort of…that is…I'm not really sure. I must go. I will be in trouble if they catch me," she shivered. "I just wanted to help. I'm suppose to be on my way to the market, so I must hurry before they close." She scurried off down the street without looking back.

"Oh, how tragic," wept Tara, "no wonder aunt and uncle never came to help us."

"Yes, it is too awful," Shalagh shuddered now crying unashamed. "I wonder why Aunt Hala did not send for us.

"She probably never received our plea for help, " suggested Tara.

"Let's leave this place," said Shalagh, attempting now to stop her tears.

They hurried to retrace their steps realizing the lateness of the hour. In an unfamiliar setting, their hearts heavy with grief, they became turned around and lost. It wasn't until much later and with difficulty the girls finally arrived at the supposed meeting place with Molly. Because they were late, Molly was not waiting for them. They were hungry and had no food and it was evident to Shalagh that Tara was feverish. Tara's cheeks were flushed and she desired only to sleep. Having no refuge, the girls returned to the place where they had stayed the night before. They had no blankets and all the cots were taken. The two girls huddled together against an inside wall until morning finally dawned.

No morning sun greeted them only a somber gray sky heavy with dark clouds. Their hearts felt just as bleak as the dark sky. For some unknown reason the soup kitchen was closed so they had no breakfast. Not knowing what else to do they aimlessly followed a small group of people, not really caring where they were going. Molly Rynn had not come for breakfast.

"I guess we were not too smart, leaving all of our belongings in the care of a stranger," lamented Tara. "All of our food and warm blankets are gone. We will probably never see her again."

"I am so sorry! " Shalagh cried out in anguish, feeling responsible for the loss of their property.

"It was a mutual agreement," said Tara trembling from the fever and the cold.

After awhile the indigent band they followed merged out into a square filled with people. Here they found themselves in the midst of the destitute and homeless. There were many children and old people, most who appeared to be ill. A large fire burned in the center of the square, but only the smoke rising into the air gave evidence of its whereabouts. The assemblage was too vast to see through or around.

"At least those who are close to the fire must have some respite from the cold," noted Tara. Her lips had turned blue and her hands and feet stiff from the frigid weather.

"Let's try to get closer to the fire," asserted Shalagh while pushing Tara ahead of her through the crowd.

"Move out of the way! Where do you think you're going?" rebuffed a thin faced woman carrying a small child.

"Get back!" snarled a bedraggled appearing older woman. "You'll not steal our place by the fire," she continued while shaking her fist violently at the girls.

Realizing the impossibility of getting anywhere near the flames of the warm bonfire, Shalagh and Tara returned to the fringe of the gathering.

"Shalagh! Shalagh Frizzle!" a shout resounded from someone just as they reached the edge of the crowd.

Looking toward the direction of the voice they eyed Molly Rynn rushing toward them.

"I have been looking everywhere for you girls," Molly smiled with relief. "We must have missed you in the line last night."

"Oh, we are so happy to see you," greeted Shalagh with a sigh of great relief.

"I would have found you somehow," declared Molly. "Your things are safe with my boys."

"We thought we would never see you again," said Tara feeling a sudden surge of renewed hope.

"I am hard to lose," laughed Molly. "Listen, we have built a fire some distance from here. It's a ways to walk, but your things are there. You have to hide provisions if you can or someone will take them away from you," she whispered cupping her hand to her mouth.

"We understand," agreed Shalagh glancing back at the grim scene they had just left behind.

"If you want to come with me, you can pick up your belongings," Molly offered kindly.

The girls agreed and were soon following Molly to the waterfront. She then led them along the frozen shoreline for some distance.

Chapter Seven

Molly Rynn chattered away as the girls made an effort to keep up with her pace. Short of stature, pretty of face with freckled complexion and reddish blonde hair, she had a rather mirthful air about her, which was rather comforting.

"We're waitin' for my husband Tony's ship to arrive," she explained. "He's been at sea for nearly a year now. He's going to be mighty upset when he learns all that has happened to the boys and me."

"Are you from Derry?" asked Tara who seemed to feel a sense of camaraderie with Molly Rynn.

"No, we had a small farm about seven miles from here. It was nearly paid for, but just before Christmas we were run off. Put us out with practically nothing but the clothes on our backs. Said we were behind on our mortgage payments. There was nothing we could do. We walked to Derry to wait for my husband. If it hadn't been for my boys, we would have frozen and starved for sure," answered Molly.

"Do you think your husband will be here soon?" asked Shalagh.

"I figure it shouldn't be too long now," said Molly. "He's going to be in a murderous state of mind when he finds out what's happened. He'll put me and the boys on the ship and take us home with him to Greece.

"But isn't this your home?" questioned Tara in surprise as she attempted to keep step with Molly.

"It always has been, but I'll be glad to be leaving it now," said Molly. "You see my husband's father was Irish but his mother was Greek. When Tony's father died his mother returned to her homeland to live out the rest of her life."

By this time, they had trudged nearly a mile along the bottom of a hill bordering the wharf. Molly continued to speak giving the girls details of the sunny farm in Greece owned by her husband's family.

"It sounds so warm," sighed Tara with a shiver.

"Yes, we'll soon be there," said Molly. "We should have left long ago, but Tony wanted to have his own farm, not work his mother's, you understand."

"Will his mother be happy to have you come?" asked Tara.

They now began to work their way up the hillside in a winding pattern.

"Yes, she has pleaded with Tony to come home for so long," replied Molly her eyes glistening wet with tears. "She's a dear soul, a bit overbearing at times, but a real caring person. Our boys are her only grandchildren. I get on with her just fine, but Tony, he gets miffed with her at times. He thinks she's too bossy. I'll just be thankful for me and my boys to have a warm place to sleep and food in our mouths while Tony is away at sea."

"How is he able to keep up a farm when he is away at sea all the time?" asked Shalagh.

"Oh, me and the boys do the farm work. But he's a bonny man," smiled Molly, "and is kind and as good as they come. It's hard for him to be away from us all the time but he makes good money. We poured it all into that farm. Now it is wasted and gone," explained Molly sadly, as they worked their way through some high overgrown dead brush along the side of the hill.

Tara slipped and nearly fell just as Molly disappeared behind some scrubby undergrowth about half way up the hill.

"Here, take my arm," insisted Shalagh as they followed closely behind Molly.

The thicket of undergrowth obscured any view from below. Sharp rocks protruded menacingly above them in a rugged disorganized arrangement which gave no access to the view from above. Here on a small shelf of level hillside some thirty or so feet above the wharf they came upon Molly's oldest son. He sat crossed legged on a wooden stool with a long gun held in the embrace of his arms. A large dog lay at his feet and growled low in its throat at their sudden appearance. Behind the boy was a crude structure put together with odds and ends of packing cases, crates, wire and miscellaneous things. A canvas was draped over the top. What appeared to be the entrance was covered with a quilt.

The boy was lanky and had the same dark good looks of his younger brother. He was muscular in frame but his face was boyish. At the sight of him holding the gun, Tara let out a shriek.

"Oh, my Lord, they are going to kill us! They are going to kill us!" she cried as she clung to Shalagh.

"Skelly, put the gun down," demanded Molly. "You scared the poor girl half to death.

"Child, it's all right," she said in a comforting tone to Tara. "Nobody is going to hurt you."

"I didn't mean to scare you," said Skelly looking at the girl. "You said to be careful, Ma and I have been watching you climb the hill and I thought you might be in danger," he explained. "They could have overpowered you."

Tara raised her head from Shalagh's shoulder just as Skelly laid the gun down and stood up.

"Skelly," said Molly, "this is Tara and Shalagh Frizzle. They have come to pick up the things we kept for them overnight."

"I'm really sorry," Skelly apologized, now smiling as he stood and stepped forward toward Tara and Shalagh to shake their hands. "I sure wouldn't hurt you."

"How's Danny?" questioned Molly, looking toward the makeshift hovel with a worried look on her face.

Before Skelly could answer, Danny pushed back the quilted door and looked out.

"Is that you, Ma? I sure am hungry. Did you find anything to eat?" questioned the boy as he hobbled out from behind the quilt with the aid of a heavy stick.

"No, I didn't," she answered, "but we'll get by somehow."

"Danny hurt his ankle, yesterday, while he and Skelly were searching for packing cases on the wharf," said Molly. "That's probably why we missed you last night, but it was all we could do to get Danny up the hill and quiet the pain in his ankle. I went back, later to find you but I couldn't."

"Is your ankle broken?" asked Tara immediately overcome with compassion.

"Naw, it's just sprained," answered Danny appearing a bit shy at the unexpected visit from the girls.

"Any sign of pa's ship?" questioned Molly scanning the rough cold water of the harbor, which was completely visible from the camp.

"No, Ma," replied Skelly.

"Well, come on in girls," welcomed Molly while grasping the quilt and holding it open.

The structure was built in the cove of the hillside with the hill itself providing three walls. The remaining wall was put together with whatever material was available, being mostly stacked packing cases. An old abandoned sail covered the top. A pit dug in the middle of the space held a fire with a cooking pot hanging over it. The canvas had been cut with an opening at the top for smoke to escape.

"Do you stay here?" asked Tara looking around her. It felt so warm in comparison to the outside.

"Yes, we do. Everything we have is here until my husband returns," answered Molly. "Here girl sit down by the fire," demanded Molly. "You look ill."

Tara gratefully obliged as she sat down on a box close by the fire. Molly quickly brought one of the fur robes and gently placed it over Tara's shoulders.

"How long have you been here?" asked Shalagh while dropping down on another box and situating herself by the fire.

"We've been here since a few days after Christmas," stated Molly. "It took some doing to put this place together and to keep it. They boys did it all. Thank the good Lord I've got them."

"Your belongings are over here," said Molly to the girls. "Will your aunt and uncle come to pick them up?"

"No," said Shalagh, "we couldn't find them."

"You didn't find them?" questioned Molly in surprise.

"No, "explained Shalagh, "we were told our uncle was dead and that our aunt died also. It would seem that our cousins were put in a workhouse."

"Oh you must think me a selfish idiot babbling on about my own self," asserted Molly, "but I thought everything was fine with you girls. What are you going to do?"

"Try to find our brothers," answered Shalagh, "and we must go to the workhouse to see about the welfare of our cousins."

"When do you plan to go?" asked Molly.

"As soon as possible, I would leave now but I think Tara is too weary and weak to walk," stated Shalagh.

They both looked at Tara who was warming herself by the fire. It was evident she could not make the trip.

"Listen girls," interjected Molly, "you were so kind to me and I would like to help you. Your welcome to stay her with me and the boys, but the truth is we have no food. We have had nothing for nearly two days, but some roots boiled in the pot and what little we can get at the soup kitchen and that's hard to come by. Now, Danny can't make the trip to the kitchen and they refuse to give extra to me. One of us must stay here on the hill or the wharf at all times. If we miss my husband's ship, he will go to the farm and not be able to find us."

"That would be tragic," asserted Tara. "How well we know with the loss of our own brothers."

"Molly," I believe that God may have brought us together for a reason. You have the means for a shelter and we have some food supplies," declared Shalagh.

"I don't understand," responded Molly.

"In the bags you and Danny brought here for us, there is more food in them than anything else," explained Shalagh.

"Oh, God be praised," blurted out Molly putting her hands to her rosy cheeks. "He hasn't forgotten us after all."

It was immediately decided the girls would stay with the Rynn's and share the food.

Shalagh then began to open the bags and remove the provisions. Molly ooed and aahed at every new discovery of food.

"Danny! Skelly!" she called, "come in here and see what blessings have fallen upon us."

They came quickly and joined into the excitement generated by the provisions.

"Shalagh and Tara, you have saved our lives," said Molly as tears streamed down her face.

Before long the aroma of bacon and cabbage filled the air as Molly and Shalagh worked side by side in the preparation of the food. Tara and Danny conversed by the fire, while Skelly went back outside to watch for the arrival of the ship as they waited for the food to be prepared. Finally, they shared a plate filled with boiled cabbage and crisp fried bacon, but before partaking of any food they bowed their heads and thanked God for his goodness toward them. Shalagh took a portion of the food to Skelly, which he promptly shared with his dog.

"I know it seems a shame to feed that dog when people are starving," said Molly, "but, he has been a faithful member of this family for a long time. He won't let nobody near us. They'd have to kill him first."

"We understand," replied Shalagh. "Will you take him with you on the ship?"

"Oh, my yes, He's my husband's dog. He'll be going with us," answered Molly, "that's for sure."

They quickly put things away as there was little to clear. They had few utensils and only two pewter plates that the girls had brought with them in their bags.

"You girls can sleep over here in the corner. Danny and me will sleep over on the other side," suggested Molly. "We've got some old quilts for beds. The bed you've got is Skelly's."

"Where will he sleep?" questioned Tara.

"Oh, he sleeps days and watches nights. He's just mixed up today because of Danny's ankle," explained Molly.

"Skelly, get in her and rest for awhile!" yelled Molly. "Danny can take your place for a few hours."

The boy came and was soon fast asleep on Molly's bed. He was up again just after dark to resume his nightly watch.

"Molly, you take one of these fur robes," insisted Tara as they were about to turn in for the night.

"I wouldn't think of it," stated Molly. "Me and the boys are used to the cold and we have made provision."

There was no talking her into it and finally with the fire glowing warm and Skelly keeping a watchful eye on everything outside they comfortably drifted off into undisturbed slumber.

Chapter Eight

Shalagh rose early the next morning, leaving Tara in the company of the Rynn's. She was determined to find the workhouse and the possible whereabouts of her cousins'. Cold and alone, it seemed she walked for endless miles. Somehow, her physical body was able to survive the rigorous journey despite the deprivation she constantly endured. In spite of her predicament she continually gave praise to God and marveled at her ability to persevere. At this particular moment, however, Shalagh had reached an emotional low. With the directions given to her by Molly, she should have reached the workhouse sometime ago. Now, she was certain she had taken a wrong turn somewhere along the way.

"Oh, Lord, what shall I do?" she whispered. Then in response to her prayer came a welcome thought to her weary mind, "trust in the Lord with all thine heart, and lean not to thine own understanding. In all thy ways acknowledge Him and He shall direct thy paths."

"I am trusting you, Lord with all my heart," Shalagh responded, "and I am certainly not leaning to my own understanding, but I am cold Lord and I am alone and lost. Please direct my path," she begged.

Suddenly, there it was a large gloomy institutional complex

of buildings, which came into view at the far end of the street. As she approached the structures a sense of foreboding came over her. How could her dear family be held in the confines of this loathsome appearing prison of a place? A bleak high iron fence enclosed the compound and separated it from the outside world. Shalagh made her way cautiously through the open gate and approached the nearest building. Timidly, she entered the main door and found herself in a comfortably furnished lobby with several chairs and small tables.

"If you are here to sign yourself in," questioned a man, seated behind a large

Desk, "you'll have to go around to the building in back. Do you have papers from the court?" he questioned assuming Shalagh desired to commit her self.

"No...no...I do not," stuttered Shalagh. "I am not here to sign myself in."

"Then what do you want?" asked the man pulling a pair of spectacles lower on his long nose and staring at the shabby condition of Shalagh's clothing.

"I am trying to find someone," explained Shalagh nervously wilting under his look of disparaging scrutiny.

"That's not our business," he spit out flatly. "I can't help you."

Shalagh wasn't to be deterred from her mission.

"Could you tell me if they might be here?" inquired Shalagh.

"Go around to the next building to the right. They might help you." He waived her off with his hand and a look of dismissal.

Shalagh went out the door and hurried to the next building. As she entered the structure on the right, conditions changed drastically. There was a tiny cubicle of a room with a makeshift desk and beyond the desk was a long hallway from which emanated a vile repugnant odor. A heavyset woman in a dirty white uniform took notice of Shalagh's arrival and started down the hallway toward her. She appeared to have been supervising two little girls who were on their hands and knees scrubbing the floor.

"You want something," questioned the coarse appearing matron. "If they sent you over from the women's quarters, forget it, we are all filled up."

"No," answered Shalagh. "I've come in search of some of my family. I was told they could be here."

"Who you looking for?" asked the woman.

"My cousins, Rylie and Bryn Frizzle," explained Shalagh. "Rylie is six and Bryn is four. They are just young children."

"Well let me take a look at the register," mumbled the woman as she pulled a thick volume from somewhere under the desk. "What did you say their names was?" she questioned while flipping quickly through the book.

"Frizzle, Rylie and Bryn Frizzle," repeated Shalagh impatiently.

"No, there ain't no body here by that name," said the woman shaking her head.

Before she could close the book and put it away, a disturbance down the hall caught her immediate attention. One of the girls had knocked over a pail of water making a loud clanking noise when it hit the floor and noisily rolled down the hallway. The matron took off in a rage screaming at the unfortunate youngster. Shalagh ducked around the desk and checked the book. It was in alphabetical order. Hastily she flipped through the pages. She could hear the sound of loud whacks being administered and cries from the child receiving them. Shalagh quickly scanned the handwritten names. Suddenly like a light shinning on the page she discovered one of the names of her quest, Rylie Frizzle listed in Unit D. Shalagh closed the book and left before the matron returned.

Having no idea of how to find Unit D, Shalagh made her way around the structure where she came upon a ragged, undernourished appearing girl. She was removing stiff, frozen articles from off a clothes line. As Shalagh approached the child gazed intently at her with large frightened eyes.

"Could you tell me how to find Unit D?" urged Shalagh softly as not to frighten her more.

There was no answer, but the girl pointed in the direction of a nearby building.

"Do you know Rylie or Bryn Frizzle?" quizzed Shalagh again gently.

Still there was no verbal reply. The youngster only shook her head and looked at Shalagh with a woeful expression.

"Thank you," said Shalagh smiling kindly at the girl.

As she turned toward the building pointed out to her she could feel the child's sorrowful eyes following her. Shalagh trembled as she pushed open the door to what she hoped was Unit D. Again a foul sickly odor nearly smothered her. She held her hand over her nose and mouth to keep from becoming violently ill. There was no waiting room, only the entrance hall in which she stood. A large framed girl, of about fourteen years of age, came down the hall toward her.

"You want something?" she inquired rudely.

"Where is the matron?" demanded Shalagh.

"She's sick and I'm in charge," disclosed the girl with a self-important attitude.

Her hair was cropped short and she had the appearance of a boy. She gave Shalagh a scrutinizing glance as she smoothed her hair with both hands back around her ears.

"I have come to visit with the Frizzle children," announced Shalagh. "Are they residing in this Unit?"

"Residing? Residing?" snorted the girl. "Well, I guess you

could call it that." And she threw back her head and vented a boisterous unsettling laugh.

"I have traveled a long way and it is most important that I see them," expressed Shalagh in a tone of authority. "I am a close relative."

"Yah, well come to think of it, there is a little girl by the name of Rylie taking a vacation with us, but she ain't allowed no visitors," conveyed the girl with a smirk on her face.

Shalagh wanted to grab the girl and shake her and maybe punch her one or two times but she controlled herself.

"If Rylie is here, why can't I see her?" fumed Shalagh.

"Orders is orders and Rylie ain't to have visitors," responded the girl, "and that is that."

She turned and started back down the hall.

"Wait a minute," cried Shalagh, "perhaps we could work something out."

The girl returned and faced Shalagh with a hard cruel smirk on her face.

"You got something we could exchange for favors?" inquired the girl with visible greed.

"I've little to give," conveyed Shalagh. "What do you want?"

"I'll take your cloak," returned the girl. "Nah, that old rag ain't worth nothing," she disclosed with further observation. "Forget it," she laughed as she started to walk away again.

"Wait!" demanded Shalagh as she reached into her pocket and produced two slices of bread with bacon in between the layers. "Will this do?" she offered holding up the tempting morsels for the girl to see.

"Is that bacon?" reasoned the girl while sniffing the air.

"Yes it is," Shalagh assured her. "Do you want it?"

Eagerly the girl returned and grabbed for the bread, her eyes bright with anticipation.

"No, it doesn't work that way," announced Shalagh, quickly pulling the desired object out of reach. Go and bring Rylie to me and the bread and bacon are yours," offered Shalagh.

The girl said nothing but left returning to the direction from which she had come. Her footsteps made a hollow echoing sound down the long hallway. Shalagh waited in anticipation, yet unsure of what to expect. Time passed. Shalagh peered nervously down the hallway. There was no one in sight. She walked back and forth in the entranceway. Then just as Shalagh was about to investigate for herself, the girl appeared gripping a frail child tightly by the hand.

"Here she is, now, give me the bread," demanded the girl in a hushed tone while shoving the child toward Shalagh. "Now, I'm going to tell you something lady," divulged the girl putting a fist in Shalagh's face. "If they catch her out here, she is done for and so am I". You make it quick, you hear me?" she threatened menacingly.

"I hear you," returned Shalagh realizing the danger of the situation.

"Now give me the bread," ordered the girl grabbing for it again.

"I must speak to her alone," declared Shalagh.

"Oh, you're pushing it," snarled the girl. "Al right, give me the bacon and I'll be just down the hall. You've got five minutes, maybe less."

Rylie stood sadly staring down at the floor. Her once beautiful eyes were now dark hollow sockets and her lovely long brown hair had been shaved tight to her head. She clasped her tiny hands tightly together in front of her ragged dress. The child's feet were bare and dirty.

"I...I am your cousin Shalagh. Do you remember me?" offered Shalagh shocked by Rylie's appearance and not knowing really what to say.

For a moment there was no acknowledgment, than slowly the child raised her head.

"You...you use to come and visit us and sometimes we would go to your house in the country. You had horses," she added brushing her hand across her smudged cheek.

"Yes, that is true," brightened Shalagh in agreement.

"Might we go there now?" asked Rylie with a sound of urgency in her voice.

"Not right now," answered Shalagh. "Rylie, where is Bryn?" inquired Shalagh.

"He is gone to Heaven," revealed Rylie showing no emotion.

"Are you sure?" gasped Shalagh.

"Yes, I am sure. They let me see him," stated the child in a soft little voice. "I saw Jesus today," announced Rylie. "He told me someone would come for me soon. He was so kind. This is a terrible place. Will you take me with you," whispered Rylie hopefully. "They are sending me to the asylum tomorrow and I do not want to go there."

Shalagh felt her heart would break for the skeleton of a child who stood so still before her. When would this nightmare ever end? Oh how Aunt Hala and Uncle Will loved this little girl and her brother. They dressed them in the finest clothes and cared for them with the greatest love and affection. Shalagh realized that if she left Rylie now she would surely die and if she took her away there was a good possibility it would still come to pass. She looked down the long hall. It was empty, not a soul in sight.

"We could go now," expressed Rylie with a look of hope.

In one quick movement they were out the door. With Rylie's hand held tight in her own they made their escape around the next building and took flight down the street. Rylie's feet fairly flew across the ground trying to keep up with Shalagh.

"Will they come after us?" yelled Shalagh down to the child.
"Yes, probably and they—they might send the dogs," stammered Rylie nearly out of breath.

"Dogs!" faltered Shalagh. "Oh, Lord Help us."

They moved from street to street zigzagging in and out as fast as Rylie could move attempting to lose anyone who might be following them. Shalagh had hoped to return to the site on the hillside before nightfall. Now she prayed for night to come quickly so they might escape into the darkness. Finally after much time they slowed to catch their breath. It was then that Shalagh realized that Rylie had come all this way barefooted. She had no shoes and her only clothing was a thin ragged dress.

"Rylie, you must be very cold," lamented Shalagh looking down at the breathless child.

"No, no, I'm not cold, let's go, they will be coming," declared Rylie nervously staring behind her.

Swiftly Shalagh loosened her shawl pulling it from around her shoulders.

"Rylie, climb on my back," she commanded as she bend down.

Rylie declined, but after Shalagh explained they could hurry much faster if she did, Rylie obeyed.

"Now, hold tight," instructed Shalagh placing the shawl over both of them and tying it tight.

They could hear voices now in the distance and the barking of dogs.

"Oh, God," pleaded Shalagh, give me the speed of angel wings and hide us from the enemy I pray."

Without looking back Shalagh took off running. She was a natural athlete, slender and graceful. Her favorite sport was riding fast horses on a race with the wind. How she wished she had one now. Night did come and Shalagh was glad. When she could run no more she walked on and on unsure as to where they were. Sometime in the night she established their whereabouts and not too long afterward stumbled onto the square. Even though the hour was late the square was teeming with the homeless and displaced. Shalagh was concerned that she could not find her way in the dark to the Rynn camp on the hillside, but she was even more fearful that whoever was pursuing them might search the crowd in the square. They left the square and begin to walk along the wharf. The sky was dark with no moon or stars to light a path. She did not know where the camp might be. After walking some distance along the wharf, Shalagh could go no farther. She was still carrying Rylie and felt completely exhausted.

"Rylie, we will stop here for the night," Shalagh told her as she slid the child gently to the cold ground. I just can't go any farther tonight. We will wrap in the shawl together until morning."

"That's all right," Rylie assured her, "as long as we don't go back to that awful place."

Suddenly a dog growled nearby. Shalagh grabbed Rylie and the child clung to her skirt, shaking with fear.

"Oh, the dogs, the dogs have found us," wept the little girl.

Then out of the dark night came the sound of a friendly voice.

"It's me and my dog," sounded Skelly's voice from right beside them now.

"Oh, Skelly, you frightened us to tears," groaned Shalagh with a great sense of relief.

"I guess I have a way of doing that," responded Skelly.

"How did you find us," asked Shalagh.

"I have been watching you coming along," he explained. "When you didn't come up the hill I figured you must not be able to find us."

"Rylie, honey, it's all right. Skelly is a friend and this is his dog," explained Shalagh. "They won't hurt us."

"Could you tell if anyone was following us, Skelly?" asked Shalagh.

"No, you were alone. I didn't even see the little girl until I got down to the foot of the hill," he stated.

Shalagh and Rylie followed Skelly up the winding trail to the camp above. Once inside the enclosure Shalagh breathed a sigh of relief. Rylie was reunited with Tara and given some warm soup. She was soon fast asleep wrapped in a fur blanket by the fire. Shalagh related as much of the days events as she could to everyone, but she too was overcome with a need for rest.

Chapter Nine

In spite of the uncertainty of the situation, morning was a happy occasion. Molly and the boys took to the tiny girl as if she were a member of their own family. Rylie appeared less frightened in the light of day and in the company of her cousins. How she had survived her ordeal was unexplainable. It was only the providence of God. Her skin was drawn tight over her tiny bones and her once beautiful curls had been shaved and bristled patches of returning hair stood up straight here and there on her scalp. Her body was covered with sores and her dark eyes sunk deep in their sockets. The child appeared to be a living skeleton.

"I am so thankful that you found her. How awful to think that she was left all alone. Aunt Hala and Uncle Will would be so pleased that you rescued her," whispered Tara. She did not want Rylie to hear her parent's names spoken.

"I am not sure whether we rescued her or not," confessed Shalagh. "What hope of any quality of life can we give her?"

"Well, at least she is away from that wretched place," declared Tara in disgust.

"I just pray we can keep her hidden from whoever is pursuing her," stated Shalagh. "With so many children in the workhouse, what is the reason for their interest in Rylie?"

"You know," said Molly, who was listening and stirring up the fire at the same time. "There is a place down on the docks where they sometimes give out used shoes and clothing to the needy. Why don't we leave Rylie in the care of Tara and the boys and see if we can get her some warm things to wear. Poor wee child with nothing to keep her protected from the cold."

"That sounds like a good idea," agreed Shalagh. "Would that be all right with you Tara?"

"Oh, yes," Tara assured them, "Rylie and I will stay here by the fire and relax."

Skelly was already sleeping rolled in his blanket in the corner. His watch was over and Danny now took up his turn sitting with the gun positioned across his legs and the dog alert at his feet. Realizing that Shalagh was leaving, Rylie suddenly stood up and clutched Shalagh's hand tightly.

"What's wrong, child," implored Shalagh. "We are only going a little way to try and find something suitable for you to wear." She patted Rylie's head gently.

"Where is my Mama?" asked the little girl staring intently into Shalagh's eyes as if to find some answer.

"I do not know," disclosed Shalagh, "I really don't."

"If she's alive, I will find her someday," proclaimed the child now with a faraway look on her face.

She never mentioned her mother again. Instead she seemed to put the thought away in some remote part of her mind reserved until a more appropriate time would permit her to pursue it.

With Molly in the lead and Shalagh close behind her they soon came upon the site where clothes were sometimes distributed to the poor. Several ragged appearing adults with children waited impatiently in front of the distribution center.

"They don't look too friendly," declared Molly while sizing up the awaiting group.

"No, I guess poverty causes people to react that way," Shalagh sighed.

Molly and Shalagh decided to wait for awhile and see if the center would open. They stood some distance away from the others. There were several ships in the harbor and they watched as great boxes and crates were hoisted on and off the docks. Passengers were boarding with excited exchanges of farewells. One ship pulled slowly away from the docks through the gray cold water amid parting shouts of goodbye. Many were crying and Shalagh could not help but wonder if Caleb and Dylan might be aboard such a ship. Still they had no money so she dismissed that thought from her mind.

"Shalagh," said Molly, "look! I think that lady is opening the door of the disbursement center. Yes, she is. She just went inside. Let's go and see if they might have anything that would fit Rylie."

Again Shalagh followed Molly as they joined a long line now quickly forming in front of the building. Many people had now gathered. The line slowly began processing through one side of the narrow structure and out the other. Suddenly a well-dressed gentleman appeared and entered in through the front door. The line came to a halt as he conversed with someone inside.

"I wonder what he wants?" questioned Molly inquisitively with some apprehension.

"He certainly doesn't need clothing," surmised Shalagh. "He is very well dressed. Perhaps he is the boss."

Some of the people waiting in line began to grumble amongst themselves. Just then the man came back out the door and proceeded to walk along the line speaking to everyone as he moved. As he came nearer to Shalagh and Molly they could hear what he was saying. It seems he was searching for a small girl of about six years of age. The child was very ill and in need of medical attention. An insane woman had kidnapped her from a nearby hospital yesterday. The little girl's uncle was very upset and was posting a large reward for her safe return. As he passed Molly and Shalagh he further explained that anyone with information about the child should contact the police or bring the girl directly to the station house. He continued on down the line and was soon out of sight.

"Well, that ought to be like finding a needle in a haystack," chuckled a woman in line behind them. There are dozens and more around here like that. I'd hate to think of how many kids are going to get dragged to the station house with a reward like that promised."

Molly reached out and squeezed Shalagh's hand assuredly. The line began to move again quickly now and as they neared the building they observed a poster that had been placed on the side of the open door. The poster read, "One-hundred pound reward for the return of Rylie Frizzle, a six year old girl who was stolen from hospital the first day of March, sadly missed by her uncle, Rogers Pierce. If found contact the local constable."

Shalagh made no comment as they were hastily shoved from behind into the narrow structure of the building.

"What do you need?" asked the man standing behind a small counter of sorts.

"I need a coat for my boy," interjected Molly before Shalagh could speak and some shoes and trousers if you got some."

Shalagh was surprised that Molly had suddenly decided on clothes for her boy.

"How old is he," inquired the man.

"Ah, he's five," blurted out Molly without any hesitation.

There were several barrels behind the counter holding used articles of clothing. Some of the things, such as shoes and boots were hung on a low hanging rope across the back of the wall.

"No, there ain't any shoes that small," he reported quickly checking to see what was available. "Here's a pair of boots that might fit, but they have a hole in the bottom of one of them."

"I'll take em," said Molly. "What about trousers?"

"Well, let me see," said the man as he rummaged through a barrel. Yep, here's a pair. Might be a little worn, but there's wear in them yet. How about this little coat, that should fit him," he said holding up the coat for Molly's inspection.

"That looks good," replied Molly smiling. "I'll take them. Would you have any stockings for a little tyke like that?"

"We just got a crate of stockings in off a ship," he explained. "Don't know what's in it."

He quickly searched through a box and came up with four unmatched stockings much too large, but better than none.

Shalagh, now breathed a sigh of relief as she realized what Molly was up to. It was much too dangerous to ask for a six-year old girl's clothing at this time. Molly had a keen sense of detecting an obvious danger. Gathering up the articles of clothing, Molly and Shalagh started on their way back to camp.

"What is it girl? You look like you've seen a ghost," quizzed Molly as they hurried along the dock.

"In a way, I feel like I have, only not directly," said Shalagh.

"What are you talking about/" questioned Molly, now becoming a little concerned about Shalagh. She hoped the girl wasn't beginning to show signs of mental problems.

"The, the name on that poster, the man in search of Rylie," stammered Shalagh.

"Yes, what about it child?" inquired Molly.

"Well, he is dead. He died a long time ago. Rudgers Pierce is my father's half-brother. He died on a ship fire many years ago."

"Are you sure?" asked Molly with surprised interest.

"Well, I am sure that Rudgers Pierce was my father's half-brother and it was always assumed that he had died in that ship fire. It has been many years and he never returned."

"Oh, mercy be, maybe someone is using his name," suggested Molly.

"But, why would he be after Rylie?" mused Shalagh questioningly.

"With all the people they have to care for, you'd think that they'd never miss one tiny little girl," sighed Molly with questioning skepticism.

"I don't know why, but I was told yesterday that Rylie was allowed no company and no one could see her. If I hadn't bribed that girl she would never have let me see Rylie," replied Shalagh.

"Well, I don't think we've got much to worry about. They'll never find her in this crowd," Molly assured her.

"I pray that you are right," said Shalagh hopefully. "Rylie could not survive if she were returned to the work house.

"I just don't know," said Molly shaking her head in disbelief. "Why would someone want to take Rylie anyway?"

"I have tried to come up with a reason," answered Shalagh, "but, until now I had not a clue."

"Did you think of something?" questioned Molly.

"I am totally in shock," replied Shalagh with a puzzled look on her face. "but, I'm wondering if someone wants the linen mills."

"I don't understand," said Molly shaking her head.

"Well, Uncle Will who is Rylie's father owned the linen mills in Londonderry. Papa sold his share in the mills some time ago. Our home of Ballymore was a business in itself and Papa preferred the farm to the mills," stated Shalagh. "Maybe Uncle Rudgers decided he wants a share of his inheritance."

"Your Papa owned Ballymore?" quizzed Molly with apparent surprise. "Oh, my that is a beautiful place. I went there, once with my husband, Tony. It was when the boys were small and Tony was thinking about taking a job in the stables. You must have been a little girl then."

"Your husband didn't take the job, I guess," said Shalagh.

"No, they hired somebody else. Tony didn't have much experience with horses. But I'll never forget that place. So that was your home...I'll be," she sighed staring at Shalagh with a greater understanding of her friend.

"It was our home," returned Shalagh sadly. "We lost it all to the bank of England. They claimed that Papa owed huge debts, but he couldn't prove that he didn't. They put us out and took it all without any explanation as to by what authority they were able to do this."

"Oh, that is terrible, but they did the same to us," stated Molly with empathy. "Said we owed them back pay. We were never behind on anything. I showed them what proof I had, but didn't do no good. They threw us out anyway."

"Well, Rudgers Pierce, for whatever reason, is not going to take Rylie away from us," declared Shalagh resolutely as they climbed the steep hill to the campsite.

"Well, I guess we're here," announced Molly.

Rylie was delighted with the offering of clothing, especially the warm stockings, although they were much too large for her. She quickly pulled a pair of them on over her cold bare feet. The stockings came up to her hips. Rylie pulled the extra pair on over the first.

"They're so soft and warm," cooed the child as she rubbed her tiny hands up and down the rough knit material.

Shalagh pulled the trousers on Rylie, tucking in the ragged dress and then rolled up the pant legs. The boots and coat were large but Rylie didn't care.

"They hold me together," laughed Rylie for the first time since her ordeal.

"Here's something to make the outfit complete," beamed Molly as she placed a wool cap of Danny's on Rylie's head. It slid down over her ears and half covered her eyes, but Rylie wore it on her head most of the time from then on.

Shalagh sat down close to the fire. She was relieved that Rylie had some clothes to wear. At least she and Molly had accomplished that. Now, if she could only find Caleb and Dylan. Where could they be hiding?

"What's wrong, Shalagh?" questioned Molly, putting a hand on the girl's back. "Anything I can do?"

"I just don't know what to do," said Shalagh. "I thought we would find Caleb and Dylan by now. I feel that we are an added burden to you and the boys."

"We'll all be fine," declared Molly. "The food that you brought with you is a life saver. I fear we would have become ill without it. I know it's hard, but, God hasn't forsaken us and He never will. No sir, we are going to get out of this predicament alive and well," she added with a determined and courageous smile on her face.

"Oh, Molly, you are a genuine optimist," laughed Shalagh, "and I love it."

Chapter Ten

The fourth week of March in 1847 the weather took a turn for the better. The frost and ice began to leave the ground as the sun made more and longer appearances. Shalagh and Tara had been in Derry since the end of February with no sighting of their brothers. They spent their days searching for food and whatever they could find to burn as fuel. What supplies Caleb had brought for them were nearly gone, even though they had severely rationed them. They relied almost totally, now on the soup kitchen of the Friends. Food was so scarce that even the soup kitchen had cut to one meal a day. Days dragged into weeks. Spring finally came but with no real relief. It remained cold and damp with little food anywhere. Skelly had brought word to the camp a few days before that someone was looking for Shalagh. Molly said that Skelly had heard it by way of the grapevine and that Shalagh had better be careful. Shalagh had responded with excitement that perhaps it could be her brothers.

On this particular day Skelly had been left to watch Rylie and the camp while the others waited in the food line of the Friends. A boy came down the line waving a message in his hand.

"Shalagh Frizzle, Shalagh Frizzle, anyone in this line by the name of Shalagh Frizzle," he repeated over and over as he moved down the line.

"Who wants to know?" yelled Molly.

"Are you Shalagh Frizzle?" questioned the boy stopping abruptly. "I have a message for you."

"Who told you to come here?" questioned Tara in a tense and irritated voice.

"I was told she might be in the food line today," explained the boy. Someone is searching for her and I have spent a great deal of time trying to find her.

Shalagh's heart was pounding. It could be a message from Caleb or it could be a trick planned by someone to find Rylie. The boy started to move away, she had to take a chance. It might be from Caleb.

"Boy, here," shouted Shalagh moving out of the line and catching up with the slim young fellow. "I am Shalagh Frizzle."

She realized she could be putting herself in great danger.

"If you be really her, than what is your oldest brother's middle name?" he questioned doubtfully.

"James, James...his name is James," answered Shalagh shaking with excitement.

The boy handed her a small envelope and quickly left without saying another word. Shalagh rejoined Molly and Tara in the food line attempting to remain calm. She nervously tore open the envelope. There was a short message inside.

"Please come to this address immediately, 543 Balmour St.," that's all it said. There was no signature.

"What is it," demanded Tara trying to see.

Shalagh handed Tara the message.

"It could be from Caleb," said Tara after reading the short note or it could be a trap to catch you and Rylie.

"What does it say?" asked Molly trying to hold back her inquisitive anticipation.

"Someone wants to meet me at that address," she acknowledged pointing to the letter in Tara's hand. "What shall I do?"

"I hate to give you advice," said Molly. "It could be your brothers or it could be trouble. But, I think you had better go and find out," urged Molly. "Rylie is safe back at the camp with Skelly and if someone is watching us, me and Danny will give them a run for their money."

"If you're going, I'm going with you," said Tara insistently. "We've got to take the chance. It might be Caleb and Dylan."

"All right than let's go!" decided Shalagh and without further thought the two girls took off up the hill and through the crowded square.

Shalagh held the message firmly in her hand and as they turned onto a main street she continued to repeat the words, "543 Balmour Street. 543 Balmour Street."

"I don't think this is Balmour Street," interrupted Tara squinting up at a street sign. "Let's ask someone where it might be."

"Sir, sir," would you be so kind to inform us as to where we might find this address?" questioned Tara of a knowledgeable appearing man walking down the street.

"What address are you looking for?" he inquired helpfully in response to her pleas.

"543 Balmour Street," stated Shalagh as she read it from the paper and held it up for him to see.

"That would be over two streets and probably down about four blacks," he explained to them pointing them in that direction. That should bring you close enough to find the address you are looking for."

The girls thanked him and hurried on, eagerly hoping Caleb and Dylan would be waiting for them. It took them another five minutes to cover the distance but soon they were standing in front of the address written in the message.

"543 Balmour Street, Harrison and Norcomb, Ticket Agents," read the large engraved sign hanging over the door.

"Ticket agents?" gasped Tara. "Why would they want to meet us here?"

"I have no idea," replied Shalagh, "but, it makes me think it probably isn't who ever is looking for Rylie. Let's go in and see what we can find out."

Once inside they found the building bustling with people. The girls stood quietly, waiting for someone to approach them.

"It looks like we will have to stand in one of those ticket lines before we can talk with anyone," noted Tara. "There certainly doesn't seem to be anyone waiting for our arrival."

"It would seem you are correct," sighed Tara. She was tired of the whole situation and wished to return to the camp. Instead they chose a line and waited for some time to pass before they approached the ticket window.

"Could I help you ladies?" inquired the ticket agent when they finally arrived in front of the window cage.

"I hope so," insisted Shalagh. "We have received a message that was delivered to us early today requesting we come to this address."

"What is your name?" he questioned.

"My name is Shalagh Frizzle," she answered softly, not wishing her name to be heard by others in line.

"How do you spell that?" he asked.

Shalagh spelled her name for him again.

"Wait here please," he requested after he had written down the spelling of her name.

He left the window and checked a long sheet of paper on the wall behind him. He then left the room returning after several minutes with another man. Shalagh and Tara were becoming very nervous. The line behind them was growing longer and this in itself made Shalagh uneasy.

"Your tickets for boarding have been approved," acknowledged the second man as he stepped in front of them.

"Our—our tickets?" mumbled Shalagh, "I don't understand."

"Your boarding tickets are confirmed for the day after tomorrow. You sail on the 'Christiana'. She's already in port," divulged the man.

"There must be some mistake," scoffed Shalagh while shaking her head in disbelief.

"Not if your name is Shalagh Frizzle," remarked the man. "A good benefactor paid for your tickets. Everything is here in this envelope."

He handed her a large brown paper envelope through the open window of the ticket cage. "The angels must be looking out for you," he smiled.

"Next?" called out the first man and the girls were forced to move out of the line to allow others to move up and take care of their business.

"Tickets, tickets to where?" muttered Shalagh holding the parcel in front of her and staring at Tara in disbelief.

"Well, I'm sure I don't know," declared Tara. "Open it up and let's see," she suggested.

"I am so disappointed," lamented Shalagh in remorse. "I was positive that Caleb and Dylan would be here waiting for us."

She clasped the oversized envelope to her and started for the door.

"I was hopeful as well, Shalagh," Tara sighed, one step behind her sister. "But don't you want to see what is in the envelope? Perhaps there is a message from the boys."

They reached the door and started down the street.

"Here, you open it," decided Shalagh shoving the envelope at Tara. "I know we've been mistaken for someone else. An error has been made. We will take the envelope back tomorrow and by then they will have realized their mistake."

"But, they had your name. That doesn't sound like a mistake to me," admonished Tara.

By this time Tara had curiously broken the waxed seal and was now pulling open the flap.

"Shalagh!" exclaimed Tara. "There are two tickets to a place called Montreal Upper Canada, wherever that may be. I have no idea," she exclaimed excitedly.

"Let me see," said Shalagh reaching for the tickets.

"That's not all," continued Tara, "there is a note," she explained holding it up for Shalagh to see.

"Open it," demanded Shalagh with renewed interest.

Tara tore open the small envelope and it read, "Shalagh and Tara, proceed immediately to Montreal in Upper Canada. Money in pouch will pay your support. You'll receive further orders upon your arrival." It was signed, someone who cares.

"Is that Caleb's handwriting?" questioned Tara as she carefully examined the penmanship of the writer of the message.

"It could be. Yes, yes, I think it is," said Shalagh. "Oh, I don't know, maybe not. I'm not sure."

"There is definitely money in this pouch," smiled Tara pulling out a small blue pouch from the larger envelope and probing its contents.

"Here, let me have it," insisted Shalagh with enthusiasm. She put the message and pouch of money back inside the large envelope and shoved them under her shawl holding them close to her body.

"We must be very careful," declared Shalagh. "Come, hurry Tara," she urged pushing ahead with a renewed burst of energy.

"Yes, agreed Tara," hurrying along side of her sister. "We could be robbed and killed for what is in that package. How much money do you think is in there?"

"We'll have to count it later. When we get back to camp," Shalagh answered gripping the envelope more tightly to her bosom.

"Do you think it's from Caleb," pressed Tara. "But, from whom would he receive so much money?"

"I have no idea," responded Shalagh crossly. "Stop asking so many questions. We need to hurry."

"But, one more thing, when did the man say we could board ship," questioned Tara.

"Day after tomorrow," answered Shalagh. "Tara, if those tickets are good, we are going to be on that ship," she said with a look of determination on her face.

"But, Shalagh, what will we do about Rylie?" questioned Tara with concern in her voice. "We can't just leave her behind."

"Then we will take her with us," said Shalagh resolutely yet with some apprehension in her voice.

"But, how will we do that?" lamented Tara. "We have no boarding pass for her and what about Caleb and Dylan. Are we going to leave the country without knowing what has happened to them?"

"In my heart, I believe those tickets are from Caleb. Perhaps they will join us on the ship. Tara, if we stay here, we shall surely die," declared Shalagh prudently. "Someone has given us the opportunity to live and it would be wrong not to take it. We have no food nor fit place to stay."

"It would appear that you are right," agreed Tara sadly, "but what about Molly and her boys?"

"We'll talk about that when we get back to camp. Let's move faster," prodded Shalagh.

Upon reaching the camp they were met by Molly who was greatly excited by something.

"Shalagh! Tara! "Molly shouted, greeting them part way down the hill. Tony's ship is in. It's sitting out there like a Greek goddess all golden in the sun." Molly was crying and laughing at the same time.

"Where is your husband?" questioned the girls caught up in the excitement of the hour.

"Oh, he hasn't come off the ship, yet," she explained. "It was Danny who saw it come into port and he came a flying up the hill to tell us. They boys have gone to wait for their father to come ashore, as he won't be expecting us to be here in Derry," she laughed unable to contain her joy.

"We are so happy for you Molly," said Tara, giving Molly a big hug.

"Our news is surprising too," said Shalagh. "Someone has purchased tickets for Tara and my-self to travel to Upper Canada."

"Then it wasn't your brothers waiting for you," said Molly with a sad glance.

"No, the address was that of a ticket agency. Our brothers were not there," explained Shalagh.

"Molly, where is Rylie?" questioned Tara as she attempted to keep the dog from jumping upon her. He had picked up the excitement of the moment and was jumping wildly about.

"Oh, the boys were so happy about their father's arrival and Rylie wanted to go with them so I let her go. I am sure she'll be fine. The boys will watch her real close. I am happy about your news, girls, but if you don't mind I'm going to join the boys on the dock," declared Molly.

"Oh, yes, that will be fine, Molly. You go and we will wait for you here," stated Tara.

Molly took off down the hill towards the wharf as fast as she could. Suddenly, Molly began to scream from somewhere below the hill. Shalagh and Tara nearly fell over each other as they half ran and half slid down the hillside toward Molly's screams.

"Rylie is gone," cried Molly as the girls caught up with her. "Someone took her just before I got down the hill."

"Who took her?" wailed Tara.

"Some men," cried the frantic woman. "Skelly said there were three of them."

"Did you see them?" demanded Shalagh grabbing hold of Molly frantically.

"No, no, she was gone when Danny met me on the wharf and told me," sobbed Molly. "Danny said she was yelling for you and Tara."

"What are we going to do?" anguished Shalagh while releasing Molly from her grip and kicking the ground in anger and frustration.

"I don't know what to do," cried Molly. "But Skelly is following them."

"How did they ever find out she was here?" demanded Shalagh. "She doesn't even look like a girl."

"Well, Danny explained that he and Skelly were trying to catch a glimpse of a small boat that had just put off from their father's ship," revealed Molly. "They just looked away for a minute and that's when they grabbed her."

"We must find her and bring her back," moaned Tara. "They will put her in the asylum for sure, or maybe worse."

Realizing the great turmoil Molly was confronted with, Tara reached out to comfort her.

"It wasn't your fault, Molly," soothed Tara, "it's the Devil at work and he's not going to win. God's on our side. Let's join hands and pray right now."

Just as they lifted their heads from praying, Skelly came running fast toward them.

"Ma…Shalagh…Tara, I followed them to where they took her," he gasped nearly out of breath. "It's a store over on Bundy Street. It looks like it has ladies hats for sale inside. But, that's where they took her."

"Oh, take us there quickly," pleaded Shalagh. "Let's hurry!"

"I'm going too," insisted Tara.

"Ma…you'd better stay here in case Danny finds Pa," suggested Skelly wiping the perspiration from his face.

"Yes…I'd better wait here," Molly agreed, "I don't want to miss him. But, you go Skelly. Hurry! Find our precious lamb."

Molly watched as they departed quickly, wringing her hands and weeping with concern.

As Skelly had explained to them it was not far to the building where the child was taken. They ran some distance along the wharf and then up the hill, scurrying past a block of tightly joined buildings. Along the way, Skelly related to them how the abduction had occurred.

"How were you able to follow them with all of these people crowded on the wharf?" asked Tara.

"Well, a woman joined them," related Skelly, "and she had on a hat with a big red feather. I could see that thing all the way through the crowd. I told Danny to go get Ma and I took off after them. I almost lost them once, but then I saw that red feather again and followed them to the place where they took her. There it is, pointed out the boy."

As Skelly had said it appeared to be a millinery shop. Ladies hats were displayed in the window. It was a fine looking shop.

"Skelly, you wait out here," decided Shalagh. "Tara and I will go inside and see if we can find anything. They know what you look like."

JOANNE C. JENSEN

No one was in the shop when they entered and all was quiet. In a minute a woman peered out from the back room.

"Do you need some help?" ladies she asked in a cordial tone. She hardly looked up as she was straightening a large red feather on a brim of a hat she held in her hand.

Shalagh lost all of sense of what to say. Quickly her eyes scanned the room. It was small with a variety of hats on display. The only doors were the one they had entered from the street and the one leading into the back room.

"We were thinking about purchasing new hats," remarked Shalagh smiling deceptively.

"You are looking for hats?" the woman sneered with a look of unbelief on her face.

She laid the hat she had been working on down on the counter.

"I don't really see what we want, do you sister?" asked Shalagh with a look of disapproval while scanning the display of hats.

"Nooo, not really," replied Tara holding her finger to her cheek.

"Perhaps, more like this one over here," stated Shalagh drawing the woman to the front window. "Yes…yes, this is more of what I had in mind. I'd like the brim to be larger though and I prefer blue ribbon for trim instead of black. Oh, but I really like this one," exclaimed Shalagh turning impetuously and taking a hat from the display. "Could you please try this one on me," she requested with a haughty air.

"My dear young lady," scoffed the woman, "this is very expensive merchandise and my clientele is the finest in Londonderry. I really think, perhaps you are in the wrong place. I might say you appearances are quite distasteful."

"Oh, is that so," returned Shalagh. "Well, for your

information, my sister and I just came into a bit of a fortune, money-wise that is, but if you don't want our business, we will be glad to go elsewhere."

In the meantime, Tara had darted into the back room while Shalagh diverted the woman's attention by taking her to the front of the shop. She was back by the time the woman turned around.

"I definitely do not care for any of these," suggested Tara stepping up beside Shalagh. "In fact, I think they are quite ugly. Too mature, you know. We will try that nice shop we saw across town."

Good idea," agreed Shalagh, with a nod of approval.

"Good riddance," muttered the shopkeeper under her breath as the girls left the store.

Skelly appeared from around the side of the building just as the girls emerged from the shop door.

"There is an alley around in the back," he half-whispered while motioning for them to follow him. "Did you find anything inside?"

"Yes, a stairway leads upstairs from the back room. They may have taken Rylie up to another floor. There is also a back door leading to the alley and they could have taken her out through it."

They rounded the building and made their way to the alley behind. The millinery shop was a three-story edifice of stone and brick. It was covered with vines.

"Be careful," cautioned Tara, "there are two windows facing the back alley from which they could probably see us."

"Might be, if I were to climb up the side of the building, I could get over to that little window on the second door," remarked Skelly studying the situation. "The wall is covered with thick vines and it seems quite sturdy."

"Perhaps you could," considered Shalagh. "Oh, but what if you would fall, it's a long way down."

"Do you think you could do it?" asked Tara eagerly. "We could give you a boost."

A more thorough examination of the vines revealed a thick and strong net of branches forming a covering on the wall.

"I think I can do it," determined Skelly, "If I could just reach the part where the vine spreads out more. Maybe I can shinny up that old pipe."

Slowly, the boy made his way up the pipe and then transferred himself to the wide-spreading vine. After a few minutes of maneuvering, he finally reached a flat roof extending out beyond a second story window. Vainly, he attempted to see inside the window, but could not see anything clearly. The window frame was stuck fast and would not open. Skelly pushed and shoved with all of his might and then suddenly it moved, nearly knocking Skelly from his position on the roof. Righting himself, he tried again. Finally, success as he struggled to open the window as far as it would go, but the opening was small and Skelly was tall. After some effort, Skelly wriggled his long body through the small opening and disappeared inside.

"Oh, I pray that Rylie is there," anguished Tara as the two girls clung together and tried to stay out of view.

It seemed as if they waited forever. Time ticked away. Just as Shalagh decided to climb up herself, Skelly appeared at the window.

"She's here," he called down in a hoarse whisper. "But, I don't know how to get her down to you."

They could see Rylie beside him now.

"I'm going up to help," said Shalagh.

"No, let me," demanded Tara. "I am lighter weight and you can lift me up to the pipe as you are taller than I am."

The urgency of the situation numbed Shalagh's thinking. She lifted Tara up where she could take hold of the pipe. Tara then scrambled up the pipe and onto the vines. By the time she got to the roof, Skelly and Rylie had climbed across the flat extension of roof to meet her. With slow cautious movement, Tara and Skelly guided Rylie down the vine, finally, dropping her into the safety of Shalagh's arms.

"Hurry, let's get out of here," muttered Skelly the minute their feet touched down in the alley.

Skelly picked up Rylie and ran toward the street with the girls closely behind him.

"They had her trussed up like a side of beef," said Skelly. "Her hands were tied up over her head to a rafter and her ankles were bound tightly with rope. They had shoved a dirty rag into her mouth."

"Oh, Skelly! How awful! I cannot believe that anyone could be so cruel to a little girl," said Shalagh in disgust as they now were mingling with crowd.

"How did you ever get her down?" questioned Shalagh.

"The ceiling was low. I couldn't stand up. I had to hunch over," explained Skelly. I pulled the dirty rag out of her mouth and she started to cry. I told her to be quiet or I couldn't help her. I untied her hands but I had a terrible time getting the rope off her ankles."

Rylie was scraped and bruised. There were red marks on either side of her mouth left by the rough gag.

"She is going to be all right now, isn't she?" questioned Skelly remorsefully who felt completely responsible for what had happened.

"I'm fine now," whimpered Rylie, clutching tightly to Tara. "They were going to take me to some uncle. I was scared and I told them I didn't have any uncle."

"Did they say your uncle's name?" asked Shalagh.

"No...no...I don't think they mentioned any names," said Rylie thoughtfully. "They just told me my uncle wanted to see me. I said I did not want to see him."

"You do not have to go," sweet child, comforted Tara. "You will stay with us."

Chapter Eleven

Reaching the wharf they faded into the crowd, where they mingled inconspicuously in order to avoid detection.

"They'll be after us," said Skelly, "as soon as they find she's gone. We've got to find some place to hide until nightfall."

"What about the camp?" Tara suggested.

"No, it's too dangerous," he an answered. "We would never make it that far anyway. If we can reach the docks I might know of a hiding place. Hurry, follow me."

Skelly led them between some huge packing cases that were stacked high ready to be laden aboard waiting ships.

"I don't think they'll be moving this stuff today," he stated. "It will give us some cover until dark."

They crept in between the cases and waited. After sometime in their cramped, cold position, Shalagh suggested to Skelly that perhaps he should go back to camp and see if it would be safe for them to return there. Everyone was tired and hungry and Skelly was eager to see his father.

"It shouldn't take you long Skelly, we'll wait here for you," stated Shalagh.

"All right, I'll be back as soon as I can," agreed Skelly as he immediately took off in the direction of the camp.

"Shalagh," whispered Tara after Skelly had left. "Do you still have the tickets?"

Shalagh felt for the envelope, "No, it's not here she gasped. Oh, Tara, what did I do with it?"

"Shalagh, you had it at the camp when Molly screamed, remember? Did you drop it?" questioned Tara.

"Oh, I may have, I don't remember, I was so upset. I think I may have dropped it on the ground by the shack," Shalagh explained. "How could I be so stupid. I must go and look for it."

"No, wait, it is my fault as much as yours," said Tara. "We were all upset. If you want to go and see if you can find it Rylie and I will be all right."

Rylie had hardly spoken a word since her rescue. She clung to Tara or Shalagh, whoever was nearest to her, terrified they would be separated.

"I'll try to hurry. Oh, what if it is gone," anguished Shalagh. "I'll be back as soon as I can. Stay down and don't let anyone see you."

Shalagh skirted around the edge of the crates, watching for officers or anyone suspicious lurking about. She hadn't gone far and was so distressed she failed to notice Skelly making his way quickly toward her in the presence of a tall muscular man.

"Shalagh," he called abruptly as she approached him.

Hearing her name she turned her head and recognized Skelly.

"This is my Pa, he was waiting for me on the dock, below the camp," said Skelly excitedly. "They got the law going through the shack at the camp. They're tearing it up looking for Rylie."

"They're at the camp now?" asked Shalagh feeling all hope was now lost of finding the envelope.

"Yes, and if Pa hadn't been waiting for me, I would have run right into them," replied Skelly.

"I am Tony, Tony Rynn, stated the man standing impressively before her.

Even in her confused state of mind, Shalagh could certainly see that Molly had not exaggerated about her husband being a bonny man. He was tall and muscular with dark curly hair, olive skin and a thick black mustache. He was dressed in a coarse woolen jacket and sailors garb.

"I take it you are Shalagh?" he smiled kindly.

"Yes, yes, I am," she stuttered feeling shy probably for the first time ever in her young life.

"Where are Tara and Rylie?" questioned Skelly.

"They are still waiting for us," explained Shalagh.

"Hurry, let's get to them now," suggested Tony. "We haven't much time. They may be watching us even now."

In a matter of minutes they arrived back at the site of the packing cases.

"This is my Pa," explained Skelly. "He's going to help you."

"Oh, I'm so glad you are back," said Tara. "Rylie has taken to crying and will not stop. She is very upset. Where are Molly and Danny? Are they all right?"

"They are now," related Skelly. "But, if it hadn't been for Pa they probably would have taken them to jail."

"It seems I arrived on the scene just in time," revealed Tony. "Someone followed my wife to the site where you had been staying and brought the law on them for harboring the child."

"Poor Molly," sympathized Tara, "she must have been terrified."

"She was," confirmed Skelly. "If Pa hadn't shown up, to take care of things I don't know what would have happened.

"Is this the child they are searching for?" questioned Tony looking down at the distraught little girl.

"Yes, and they could find us at any moment and take her

away," lamented Shalagh. "We have no place to go. I do not know what to do."

"That is what I've come to tell you," divulged Tony. "Molly found your boarding passes. According to what she said, you are to sail the day after tomorrow, is that right?" he inquired as he handed Shalagh the lost envelope.

"Yes, oh thank God," breathed Shalagh and Tara simultaneously.

"Thank you so much. I thought we had lost them for good," said Shalagh with a sigh of relief.

"That's all right," declared Tony, "it seems you girls and my Molly and the boys have gone through a terrible ordeal together. I can't believe the situation my family has been put into and made to suffer."

"It was our good fortune to have found each other," said Shalagh. "But, I do not know what we will do until we can take passage on the ship. Where are Molly and Danny now?"

"They are safe. I put them on board my ship along with old Raider the dog. Listen girls," clarified Tony, "the Christiana may not sail until the day after tomorrow. But the ship is in the harbor, now. Perhaps you could board it sooner. Best thing for you girls to do is to take that child and get on that ship. It would probably be last place anyone would look for her."

"Oh, do you think that could be possible?" Tara implored. "Could you give us any advice of how we could board the ship?"

"We are forgetting something," interjected Shalagh with a shake of her head. "We have no boarding pass for Rylie."

"You may not need one," offered Tony. "I know the first mate of the Christiana. He is a friend of a friend of mine."

Shalagh sensed a small feeling of relief as Tony's words

began to give her renewed hope. Perhaps they could make it to the safety of the ship, but what then? They had been told of the horrible atrocities that took place aboard some of these "death trap" ships. Still they had no choice. If they stayed they faced starvation for sure and possible imprisonment. They had no choice but to go.

"How can we find the ship and what do we have to do to board it?" questioned Tara. She was desperate to get Rylie off the street.

"I think I can help you," stated Tony. "This could be the ideal time to leave here as they may think you will stay in hiding until dark."

It was now well into the late afternoon. The sun had given way to dark snow clouds and a damp cold wind had picked up from the north.

"Perhaps you are right. We should leave here now," agreed Shalagh.

"Let's do something," pleaded Tara while desperately trying to comfort Rylie. Tara herself was feeling ill with fever.

"Shalagh, if you and I could walk together and carry Rylie, it might appear that we are a couple out for a walk," suggested Tony. "Tara and Skelly could follow a little ways behind. But do stay close," he advised.

So it was agreed upon. Rylie offered no fuss as Tony lifted her in his strong arms and held her tight.

"Here, Shalagh, hold on to my arm. It will be more convincing," he instructed.

Shalagh's heart throbbed within her breast and she flushed at the thought, but she did as Tony suggested. They left the security of the packing cases with Rylie settled in Tony's strong arms. He was so big and Rylie so small that she was hardly noticeable nestled comfortably there. Shalagh held tightly to

Tony's arm, fearful that any moment they would be confronted and Rylie snatched from them.

"Try to relax a little. Do not appear so frightened," suggested Tony smiling down at Shalagh. "Just pretend we are taking a stroll together along the wharf." He commenced to hum a little tune to further allay her apprehensions.

Shalagh sensing Tony's strong support and fearless demeanor began to relax and comply with his request by being calm and composed. Her thoughts momentarily switched to Caleb and Dylan wondering where they might be.

"Molly will be sailing with you?" asked Shalagh.

"Yes," affirmed Tony assuredly while adding, "she's the love of my life."

"I am so happy for both of you and your family," confessed Shalagh. "When does your ship depart for Greece?" inquired Shalagh.

"As soon as we unload our cargo," he explained, "and I will take Skelly with me to the ship."

"Then we will not see Molly or Danny again," murmured Shalagh sadly. "Will you please tell them we will miss them and that it was a great pleasure to have known them?"

"I will," he answered with a smile, than interrupting himself as he looked toward the sea, "There she is," declared Tony suddenly, "the Christiana, she's anchored out a ways."

"Oh, it is so far away. How will we ever get to her?" asked Shalagh. "Why is she out so far?"

"It is too easy for refuges to jump ship," replied Tony. "They're bringing their cargo back and forth in large rowboats to avoid taking on stowaways."

Skelly and Tara caught up with them just as the last rays of the light of day faded away.

"Wait here," demanded Tony suddenly thrusting Rylie into

Shalagh's arms. "Skelly, come with me," he added as he took off leaving the girls standing on the dock alone.

"Where is the ship?" inquired Tara as she peered off over the dark water. She was shaking, now, with fever.

"It's out there some distance," responded Shalagh. "It appears to be rather small."

"How will we ever get out to that ship?" asked Tara in dismay.

"I have no idea, but Tony said to wait here," Shalagh answered.

Darkness descended rapidly and with it a heavy fog. The girls waited in the black silence unsure as to when Tony would reappear. Every sound brought fear to their hearts. It seemed like an eternity since Tony had left.

"Maybe they can't find us," offered Tara. "It's so dark and foggy and it seems like a long time since they had left."

"Wait," cautioned Shalagh, "I think I hear something. Be still. Rylie stop crying, please."

Then out of the heavy fog came the sound of splashing oars against the frigid waters. Someone gave a shrill whistle and a small boat slipped out of the dark and scraped the side of the pier. Out of the mist appeared a man who leaped from the boat and quickly secured it.

"This is my friend, Clancy," introduced Tony pointing to a man seated on a plank in the center of the boat. He will take you to the Christiana. Hurry girls," Tony insisted.

Skelly stood up in the boat and offered a helping hand to assist the girls in entering the small craft rolling with the incoming waves. The girls were so stiff with the cold that it was difficult for them to maneuver. Finally, they were seated in the rear of the boat.

"Take good care of them, Clancy," said Tony. "Come Skelly, we must go," he insisted.

121

"Wait a minute, Pa," Skelly begged. Then he bent and hugged each of the girls bidding them goodbye. "I will see you both again someday," he said hopefully. "Take care of yourselves."

"Come on, Skelly," repeated Tony. Skelly jumped free from the boat and the two of them slipped away into the darkness.

It took them a good half an hour to reach the Christiana. Clancy said little as the wind was blowing the black water into rough waves causing him to row hard in order to keep on course with the ship. At times it seemed that they went backwards more than they went forwards. Cold water splashed over the side and into the small boat. Tara felt she could not take much more. Her fever was spiraling and they all needed rest and food.

"Nothing to fear," yelled Clancy over the noise of the wild and churning water. We'll be on board the Christiana before you can say scat."

Shalagh wasn't so sure of that. She could see little in the dark, but now the wind had come up strong and was beginning to blow the fog away. It was still too dark to see anything and a cold icy rain begin hitting their faces.

"Looks like she's blowing up a storm," shouted Clancy.

"Wonderful," said Shalagh resolutely, "that's all we need."

All of a sudden the Christiana loomed upon them out of the black rolling sea. Shalagh had no idea how Clancy was able to come upon it. The ship was much larger than she had thought. It appeared much smaller from a distance.

"Ahoy, up there you mates," shouted Clancy with his hands cupped to his wet cheeks.

A voice resounded from somewhere above, "Ahoy, who goes there?"

"Clancy, pull us up!" he commanded.

Lines were quickly dropped and secured on the small boat

and then they were skillfully hoisted up the side of the vessel onto the wooden deck. Once on board, Clancy took a lantern from one of the sailors who had pulled them up to the deck.

"Watch your step ladies, it's wet and slippery," cautioned Clancy. "Follow me," he shouted into the howling wind swinging the lantern high so they could see to follow him.

It was difficult to hear as the storm began to pick up momentum. Clancy pulled open a door and they followed him inside and down a couple of steps. They had entered a short corridor with a door standing open at the other end. Once through the open door, they arrived at a rather large rectangular room with a long table in the middle, surrounded by chairs. The room was well lighted by secured hanging lanterns and Shalagh could see there were five or six closed doors leading off from the room. They could hear voices coming from somewhere close by. Clancy now opened one of the doors.

"Your cabin is just a few steps down the hall," he directed while ushering them through the door. "Someone will be along shortly to see about your supper."

After they were safely inside, his work accomplished, Clancy closed the door and left. The soft glow of an oil lamp lighted the small chamber. The walls and ceiling were of a light knotty wood. A tiny stove burned warmly in one corner. A double-deck bunk bed took up most of one wall while a built-in wash stand at the far end completed the room.

"Oh, Shalagh," exclaimed Tara, "a bed, a real bed," and she rolled herself onto the bottom bunk, "with pillows and a soft comforter. This is too good to be true," she added brushing her hand across the soft material of the bed cover.

Rylie joined Tara, stretching her wasted little body out to mimic Tara's position on the bunk.

"A real pillow," she said comfortably positioning her head upon it.

Shalagh leaned wearily against the closed door. This was not at all what she had expected. This was indeed nice, warm, comfortable and private. They had a real roof over their heads instead of a canvass and surrounded by solid walls for their protection.

"This is very, very good," proclaimed Shalagh.

Before anyone could speak again, a knock sounded on the door.

"May I come in?" called out the throaty sound of a woman's husky voice.

Shalagh opened the door and stepped aside as a tall woman with a weathered looking complexion entered the room. Although she was attired in men's rough clothing, she appeared to be rather attractive in the shadowy light.

"I brought you the victuals myself," she explained. "We haven't had passengers for quite a spell. I wanted to see what you looked like," and she laughed a hearty laugh.

She carried a large tray covered with a red and white checkered cloth.

"Let's set the water pitcher on the floor," she suggested, "then I can put the tray on the wash stand."

Tara and Rylie had jumped up off the bed when the knock came on the door. They quickly remove the water pitcher and bowl, placing them on the floor.

"Thank you, dears," smiled the woman as she set the heavy tray on the table.

The wonderful aroma of food filled the room and sent the girls mouths to watering.

"It's just leftovers," the woman apologized. "We've got hardy men aboard this ship and they like to eat, so we give them plenty of just plain food."

"Whatever you brought will be greatly appreciated," returned Shalagh not sure quite when they had last partaken of food.

"Yes, I think I could eat the tray," said Tara while breathing in the delicious aroma.

" I mean I am that hungry," she explained now feeling a little silly about her statement of being able to eat the tray.

The woman observed Tara's white face and sunken feverish cheeks with a look of concern.

"Well, I've got to get back to work," she told them. "I just wanted to say, welcome aboard. My name is Annabelle. I am Captain Logan's wife."

Annabelle started to leave but turned to explain that there were extra blankets in a compartment under the lower bunk.

"Oh, by the way," she added, "breakfast is at eight bells. We eat in the dining hall. I'll be back to pick up the tray later."

As Annabelle shut the door, Tara took one short leap and quickly removed the cover from the tray. What a feast, they had not seen such fine food since they left Ballymore. There was ham and gravy with biscuits, butter and jam and a pot of hot tea. There was a small pitcher of milk and Tara was nearly overcome with delight at the sight of a fruit cobbler. Annabelle had not forgotten a thing. There were plates and silverware, cups and napkins. They devoured the food in silent enjoyment until they could hold no more.

"I really don't believe that I ever had better food in all my life," declared Tara with a full feeling of satisfaction.

"Nor I," agreed Shalagh. "Nor have I ever eaten so much."

"What kind of sailing vessel is this?" questioned Tara in wonderment. "We have heard such terrible things about the ships that carry passengers away from here."

"This does not appear to be one of those," Shalagh assured

her. "Did I understand Annabelle to say that they do not carry passengers often?"

"That is what she said," voiced Tara affirmatively. "Oh, look," she interjected lowering her voice to a whisper and pointing to Rylie on the lower bunk.

Rylie had fallen to sleep on the bottom bunk. She was curled up on the comforter and a tiny bit of color showed in her pale cheeks.

"Let's pull her boots off," suggested Shalagh.

Together, they removed Rylie's boots, damp dirty stockings and her coat. They covered her with a warm blanket from under the bunk. Just then Annabelle knocked on the door again. On admittance she entered with some folded articles of clothing.

"Here, I thought you might need these to keep warm," she offered. "I couldn't help noticing you have no baggage. If you'll put your outer garments outside the door, I'll see to it they get washed."

It was then that Annabelle noticed Ryliie asleep on the bed.

"Precious little angel," she whispered as she backed out the door, closing it carefully.

The folded articles proved to be warm nightgowns complete with nightcaps. They were probably Annabelle's own gowns as they were long and large and Annabelle was tall and strong of build.

"I don't understand how she could accomplish the task of getting these rags we are wearing, washed and dry by morning," remarked Shalagh.

"Well, let's do as she asked, anyway," said Tara with a big yawn.

They changed into the nightgowns and placed their tattered and folded clothes outside the door. Shalagh took the top bunk, while Tara cuddled up close to Rylie on the bottom bunk. They soon became oblivious of the roll of the ship and the howl of the wind outside. Exhaustion gave way to the warmth and soft comfort of their beds.

Chapter Twelve

Gong, gong, gong sounded the ringing of the ship's bell interrupting Shalagh abruptly from a sound sleep. The rolling of the waves against the hull rocked the ship in a constant up and down motion. Slowly, the events of the day came back to her. For a few moments she lay there with the comfort of the warm blankets wrapped snugly around her. After awhile she raised up enough to look over the side of the upper bunk and glance down to the one below. Tara and Rylie were still asleep. It was such a relief to know that they were warm, comfortable and safe. She wondered if their clothes had been laundered and replaced outside the door as Annabelle had promised them. Annabelle had stated that at eight bells breakfast would be served in the dining salon. Shalagh wasn't sure how many bells she had heard when she awoke. Carefully she slipped one foot over the edge of the bunk, then the other and attempted to slide noiselessly to the floor. The nightgown that Annabelle had supplied was large and comfortable but it was very long. Shalagh had to gather it up around her waist to keep from tripping as she crossed the cabin to the door. The fire in the tiny stove had either gone out or was burning low and the room felt chilly. In spite of Shalagh's care in opening the door it made a squeaking noise as she turned the knob and pulled it toward her.

Rylie stirred in her bed but Tara slept on. The door creaked loudly as she pulled it wide open, but still the two did not awake.

A parcel wrapped in brown paper had been placed outside in the hallway. The immediate door to their room opened into a tiny entrance with an adjoining door which led directly into the dining area. Shalagh could hear the sound of men's voices and the clatter of dishes. She picked up the bundle and carried it inside. Upon opening it she discovered the contents were not the same articles they had placed there the night before. Instead the package held two crisp white blouses, two woolen skirts, warm underclothing and two wool jackets with thick linings. Shalagh hadn't included Rylie's clothes to be laundered as Rylie had fallen asleep in what she was wearing. The package held nothing for her. About this time, Rylie rolled over and looked up at her.

"What's all that stuff?" she asked rubbing her eyes sleepily.

"I guess Annabelle sent us some clothes," explained Shalagh.

"Is Annabelle the lady who was here last night?" questioned the little girl.

"Yes, she came twice last night, but you were asleep. Did you sleep well?" asked Shalagh.

"Uh-huh," replied the child. "Tara is still sleeping."

"I am awake," sounded the muffled voice of Tara from under the blankets pulled over her head.

"Annabelle left us some clothes to wear," explained Shalagh exposing the contents of the package. "I heard the sound of voices when I went to retrieve them from the hall. I think they are having breakfast now."

"I'm hungry," stated Rylie emphatically.

"After all you ate last night?" declared Shalagh.

"Can't help it," laughed Rylie.

"Oh, Rylie, it's so good to hear you laugh," returned Shalagh enthusiastically. "Let's find out if we can still get some breakfast. Oh my, before we do, we should try and wash up some or they might not let us in the salon," suggested Shalagh.

A drawer in the wash stand contained soap and towels, a hairbrush and comb. A mirror was fastened on the wall behind the stand. A pitcher set in a wash bowl held a small amount of water.

While Rylie performed a hurried wash job with the cold water Shalagh brushed her own hair. She then attempted to do something with Rylie's. The child's hair had now grown out to about a quarter inch in length. The sever manner in which it had been cut caused it to stand straight out in a peculiar fashion all over her head. Adding to it all, Rylie had sores on her scalp caused from malnutrition and it was painful to have her hair brushed. Rylie's skin was drawn so tight from starvation that it gave her a haggard look of old age. The pain was too great when Shalagh attempted to comb Rylie's hair so they patted it down with water.

"I look scary," said Rylie standing on tiptoe to stare into the mirror.

Tara who had uncovered her head was watching from the bunk.

"I think you look real nice, Rylie," she comforted.

"Tara, are you coming? I am almost dressed," stated Shalagh while donning the blouse and fastening the skirt around her waist.

"I'm awfully tired," replied Tara.

"I know," said Shalagh, "but, you need something to eat."

Shalagh walked over and felt of her sister's forehead. It was hot with fever. It was difficult to know what was best for Tara.

She realized her sister needed special care if she were to survive, as did Rylie, care that she could not presently give them. Not wishing to upset Tara, Shalagh pulled more blankets from the top bunk and tucked them gently around her feverish sister. At least Tara was warm and protected here.

"We'll be back soon," stated Shalagh. "See if you can sleep. We will get you some breakfast."

"Thank you," responded Tara as her head sank weakly into the comforting folds of the pillow.

There were only two men seated at the long table in the dining salon when Shalagh and Rylie entered the room. The younger appearing of the two said good morning while the other simply nodded his head as he looked in their direction. The men finished eating and left soon after the girls arrived.

"Good morning, misses," uttered the sound of a friendly voice from the open pantry door just off the dining area. A gentleman of Chinese origin greeted them with a happy smile on his face.

He was very trim and short of stature with fine oriental features. He was dressed in typical Chinese apparel except for his steward's jacket, which was spotlessly white. He was extremely neat in appearance.

"My name is Mr. Lee," he introduced himself with a curtly bow. "We've flapjacks, coffee and sausage and milk for the little one. Sit down anywhere you'd like," he motioned as he glanced with sad eyes at Rylie.

The girls found a place at the end of the table. As Mr. Lee turned towards the pantry, to Rylie's amazement, there was a long, thick and black braid of hair falling from the back of his head all the way to the floor. She made no comment but, passed a look of surprise to Shalagh.

In no time at all, Mr. Lee brought out a platter piled high with hot pancakes and sausage. He went back to the pantry and returned with a hot pot of coffee, a pitcher of milk and some syrup and jelly.

Shalagh thought of Tara.

"Mr. Lee," she ventured as he poured hot coffee into a cup beside her plate. "My sister is not feeling well this morning. She is in her room. Would it be possible for me to take her some of these pancakes and perhaps some coffee with milk?"

She waited, half-fearing what his response might be after all they were late for breakfast. Mr. Lee smiled a broad smile and left the room disappearing into the pantry.

"Maybe he didn't understand," reasoned Shalagh. She glanced at Rylie who was happily piling pancakes on her plate and dredging them in syrup.

"Probably not," agreed Rylie as she took a big bite and reached for the sausage, " but, we can take her something."

"If there is anything left when you finish eating. Rylie, don't eat so fast. You are going to be sick," admonished Shalagh gently.

The child slowed her rapid pace of gouging food but still continued to eat with gusto. Before Shalagh could fill her own plate, Mr. Lee exited from the pantry. He had prepared a tray of the same delicious food that was placed before them. He had added a pat of butter and some tea cakes.

"Will this be all right?" he asked waiting for Shalagh's approval before he covered the tray with a large white linen cloth.

"I am so obliged to you," responded Shalagh. "I will take it to her now. Thank you, Mr. Lee."

"Tell missy to keep the tea cakes in her room to snack on," he added as Shalagh arose to go.

Rylie jumped up to follow. She enjoyed the food, but she

would not let Shalagh out of her sight. Tara was awake and so grateful for the ample breakfast. She asked Shalagh to send her thanks to Mr. Lee for the delicious food and especially for the tea cakes.

Shalagh and Rylie returned to breakfast alone in the cozy warmth of the dining salon. They could hear Mr. Lee singing a hymn in the adjoining room as he worked. Once he came to the door and waved at them. Rylie continued to eat, but slower and slower, refusing to stop. She was ever fearful it would be her last bit of food.

"Do they have cows here?" Rylie questioned Shalagh, as she drank the last of the milk.

"I doubt it," replied Shalagh shaking her head at the very thought of it.

A few minutes later Mr. Lee brought in some fresh coffee.

"Mr. Lee," inquired Shalagh, "Rylie would like to know where the milk comes from?"

"Milk," repeated Mr. Lee. "Milk, oh, ha-ha, yes, well you see we have goats on board. Pity and Patty are their names. We give them grain and they in return give us milk and butter. Good deal, huh?" he winked at Rylie.

Rylie put her head down shyly.

"We keep chickens, too," he added appearing very proud of their achievements. "We make you fat," he laughed and returned to his work.

Finally, Rylie could hold no more. She found herself unable to partake of even one more morsel. It was then that Annabelle joined them.

"I'm back, Mr. Lee," she greeted, "and I could sure use a cup of your coffee right about now. Did you girls have enough to eat?" asked Annabelle while seating herself at the table near them.

"Yes ma-m, we surely did," affirmed Shalagh.

"Well, it's going to take some doing to plump this child up," noted Annabelle. "They tell me it's a common sight on the isle. But we don't see much of it from the ship. Thank goodness," she murmured. "Looks to me like you and the other girl could take some plumping too." Annabelle shook her head at how thin they were. "The other girl is your sister I'm told, is that correct?" asked Annabelle.

"Yes, she is my younger sister," Shalagh informed her. "We call her Tara, but her name is really Taryn."

"And, this one," questioned Annabelle, "who might she be?"

"This is our cousin, Rylie," introduced Shalagh. "I'm sorry you did not meet her last night. My name is Shalagh Frizzle. I think we were just too exhausted to be polite. It was my thought that you were told who we were and the person who was responsible for our passage."

"No, I only knew we were taking on passengers," clarified Annabelle. "Two young girls is what my husband told me. I didn't know about the little one until Clancy the first mate explained to me it had all been arranged," she said smiling kindly at Rylie.

Rylie smiled shyly back. Her unruly hair was sticking straight up again. The pants and shirt she had worn constantly since the day they were given to her did not add any good thing to her appearance.

"We'll see if we can do something about your outfit," remarked Annabelle. "By the way, where is your sister this morning?" she inquired while cautiously sipping the hot coffee Mr. Lee had brought her.

"She wasn't feeling well. Tara is very tired so she remained in the cabin," explained Shalagh. "I hope that's all right."

"What?" quizzed Annabelle looking questioningly at Shalagh. "Why, yes dear, the cabin is yours for the duration of the trip. I thought that child looked awful pale last night."

"It's been very difficult for her," disclosed Shalagh. "We've been moving about for some time now. She really needs rest and nutritious food."

"Well, she'll get plenty of both here," declared Annabelle slapping the table with her hand signifying her complete agreement. "They'll be nothing much to do but rest for probably for the next six weeks or so."

"We'll be on shipboard all that time?" inquired Shalagh with a look of surprise.

"I'm afraid so, maybe longer. We're heading out of here as soon as the wind is right. We brought in a full supply of food for the refugee's and now we will return to Liverpool to take on our cargo. From there we'll sail for upper Canada," reported Annabelle.

"I see," reasoned Shalagh.

Shalagh was convinced that Annabelle knew nothing about the mystery of who had paid for their passage. She wondered if Caleb and Dylan might be working on this ship. Annabelle probably would not know who they were. Perhaps she could find out later on.

"I think I had better go and check on Tara," remarked Shalagh. "I don't like to leave her alone too long."

"Would you mind if I tag along and have a look at your sister?" requested Annabelle. "I'm the only doctor this ship has."

"Are you truly a doctor?" asked Rylie speaking for the first time in Annabelle's presence.

"No, not really," laughed Annabelle. "That is, I don't have a degree, but I've done a lot of caring for the sick in the years we've been at sea. Yep, I can set a broken leg, pull a tooth and give you the right medicine for what ails you for most of the time."

"Is that your official job aboard ship?" questioned Shalagh.

"Lands no," chuckled Annabelle, "I'm the navigator. Captain Logan, he's my husband, and we've been sailing for near unto ten years together now. The cabin your girl's are sharing belonged to our daughters. The oldest one met and married a landlubber nearly three years ago. Nice fellow, though, although I wouldn't admit it to him. I'm going to be a grandma before we get back," she beamed. "Our oldest is due any day now. Can hardly wait to see that little one. We've been gone a long time," explained Annabelle. "We sailed out of Quebec with a full load last August, unloaded and wintered over in Barcelona. Captain got word of trouble here and brought in a load of supplies three days ago."

"Where is your other daughter," asked Shalagh as they arose and walked toward the cabin.

"We left her home in York. She wanted to go to school there. It's hard, me trying to teach her here on the ship. Not much for a young girl to do either. She loved the sea though, but we left her with her sister and brother-in-law," explained Annabelle.

They had reached the cabin now and Shalagh knocked gently on the door.

"Who is it?" quizzed Tara's soft voice.

"It's me, Tara. I've brought Annabelle to see you. Is it all right if we come in?" she requested.

"Yes, please do," Tara answered. "I guess I fell back to sleep after breakfast. It was so good. Thank you."

"Do you feel any better," asked Rylie climbing in beside Tara who was now sitting up in the bunk.

"I believe I do," stated Tara.

"Annabelle is kind of the ship's doctor and she wanted to take a look at you. Do you mind?" questioned Shalagh.

"Why, no," said Tara, "I guess not."

Given permission, Annabelle proceeded to ask a few questions, check for fever, looked down Tara's throat and thumped her upper back and chest.

"Young lady," commented Annabelle after a few more minutes of observation, "it is my opinion that you need several days of complete bed-rest. We must get rid of that fever. We will be pouring a lot of liquid and food down you. I've got a tonic and some medicine in my quarters. We'll start you on it right away. If you cooperate, I believe we can soon make you well again."

Tara offered no argument. She allowed Annabelle to have a bath drawn for her. While she was out of the room, Mr. Lee put fresh linens on the beds, built up the fire in the tiny stove and brought fresh drinking water for the pitcher on the stand. When Tara returned to the room, Annabelle gave orders for both doors leading, to the small stateroom be left open to allow for the air to circulate.

"No one will bother you girls here," affirmed Annabelle. "Nobody is allowed in here but the captain, my-self and Mr. Lee. Mr. Lee will do all the straightening up and bring your meals to you, honey. He'll keep the fire warm, but he won't bother you none. If you hear anyone else about, it's just Clancy, the first mate. He's the one who brought you here last night," said Annabelle. "There's also Will and Swede the second and third mates. They get a little loud with their talking sometimes when they're in the dining room, but they're not allowed back here. This was our girl's room and if they even thought of stepping in this direction, my husband would have thrown them overboard to the fish."

Rylie appeared a little upset at Annabelle's statement about throwing them overboard. She certainly did not want the same peril to befall her.

"Don't worry child," assured Annabelle sensing Rylie's fear. "Captain Logan has never thrown anyone overboard. Besides, you couldn't find more trusting mates than we have on board the Christiana."

"What kind of ship is this?" questioned Shalagh as she and Annabell made Tara more comfortable in the fresh linens of the bunk.

"She's a clipper," smiled Annabelle, "named for our girls, Christy and Tiana." We usually carry cargo, very rarely passengers."

Shalagh felt uncomfortable to question any further and dropped the subject.

Annabelle took a final check of the cabin, making sure everything was pleasant and comfortable for her patient.

"I will look in on you later," she explained. "Right now I'm going to my quarters for some medicine. Why don't you two girls follow along," suggested Annabelle to Shalagh and Rylie.

Chapter Thirteen

The girls obediently followed Annabelle out into the small hallway.

"We'll see if we can find something for Rylie to wear. I have a few of my daughter's things left in a trunk in my cabin. I doubt if there's anything small enough for you though. It's been a long time since my girls were that small. Matter of fact, I don't think they ever were," laughed Annabelle.

Annabelle took the lead through the mess salon. She gave a quick explanation of how the mess table was built around the mizzenmast. The table was fitted with racks to prevent dishes from sliding off its surface. The swivel dining chairs were fastened to the deck to keep them from shifting.

"The mate's and steward's cabins are the doors off to the right," she motioned as they crossed the dining hall.

Annabelle walked through an open door at the end of the mess hall into what she called the parlor.

"The men call it, the salon," she snorted. "It's a parlor to me."

The walls of the parlor were fitted with rare wood and mirrors. There were sofas built against the wall on two sides and a table secured in the middle of the floor with two overstuffed chairs beside it. The color scheme was predominately red. A large overhead skylight allowed daylight to flow into the room making it light and airy.

"You can call this home while you are on this ship," offered Annabelle. "The men use it some, but they're too busy most of the time especially when we are at sea."

The men referred to were the Captain, first, second and third mate's and the steward. The rest of the crew lived in the forward or mid section of the ship. They were not allowed below deck in the clipper's stern except in an emergency.

At the far end of the so-called parlor, Annabelle opened another door leading into a narrow hallway.

"To your right is the bathroom," Annabelle gestured. "You can use it anytime you want. Just knock before you enter. If you want to bathe let Mr. Lee know as the water must be heated and poured."

Annabelle now opened a door on the left of the hall across from the bath chamber.

"This is my home away from home," conveyed Annabelle. "Come on in."

The large stateroom was equipped with a desk, sofa, washstand, closet and an over sized bunk. There was a bright patchwork quilt on the bunk and a knitted Afghan was thrown across the sofa. Books lined the back of the desk. Annabelle walked over and opened a large trunk near the bunk. She rummaged through the contents finally coming up with a few articles of clothing she thought Rylie might be able to wear.

"This is like a house isn't?" observed Rylie walking around the room and touching everything of interest.

"Yes, it is our home," disclosed Annabelle. "Later, I'll take you girls up on deck. We had a storm last night and it's pretty wet and cold out there now. But, let us first take this medicine back to Tara. After that, you girls can entertain yourselves in the parlor until dinner if you want. There are some books on the table which may interest you."

Shalagh and Rylie followed Annabelle back to Tara's room where she quickly administered the tonic and medicine.

"Here, Shalagh, Tara must have her medicine after every meal," stated Annabelle. "I'll just leave it here on the table. I've got to get back to work now, but if you need anything, Mr. Lee is never too far away from the kitchen. Mr. Lee is our steward and faithful friend."

"Oh, Mrs. Logan," said Shalagh, "if you wouldn't mind, I might be able to alter some of the clothes you found for Rylie. I've had quite a bit of experience in sewing. We were taught in school."

"Good," replied Annabelle, "I'll just put these things in the parlor for you. And please call me Annabelle," she requested with a smile. "Everyone around here does."

For the remainder of the voyage, the girls called her Annabelle. Her rough exterior appearance was only the wrapping. Underneath was a kind and generous lady. She could put a rowdy sailor in his place without a moment's hesitation. Her word was law and the crew highly respected Annabelle. She would accept nothing less.

The morning passed swiftly as Shalagh worked on the articles of clothing left for her in what Annabelle referred to as the parlor. There were a couple of blouses, which were much too large along with a skirt and dress. Annabelle had also left a sewing box filled with threads of various kinds and colors, a pair of scissors and buttons. By the time the dinner hour rolled around, Shalagh had managed to cut and stitch the dress to sort of fit Rylie's minute proportions. Shalagh and Rylie had checked on Tara several times but on each occasion found her to be sleeping. Just before the dinner bell rang, however, they found Tara awake.

"It's almost dinner time," said Rylie, "and it sure smells good."

"We'll bring you a tray," stated Shalagh.

"I think I feel well enough to join you," decided Tara sitting up in bed.

"Well, if you would like to," replied Shalagh. "But, Annabelle said for you to stay in bed."

"Perhaps I should then," considered Tara remembering with what authority Annabelle had spoken.

Dinner was a delicious stew with dumplings. There was tea with milk and some sort of a biscuit like cookie with a raisin sauce. Annabelle did not come to dinner, only the second mate, Mr. Olsen. He talked a great deal and told to them amusing stories that made Rylie laugh. A check on Tara after dinner found her comfortable and dozing again.

"Shalagh, is that you?" questioned Tara just as she and Rylie were tiptoeing out the door.

"Yes, how are you?" asked Shalagh reentering the room.

"Comfortable," responded Tara, "I just seem to be so tired. I keep falling asleep."

"Annabelle explained that the medicine she gave you would make you sleepy," explained Shalagh. "You need to relax and rest so that you soon will be well again."

"I'm really quite content to lay here and do nothing," replied Tara. "It's just that I feel that I'm such a bother to everyone."

"Dear Tara," responded Shalagh, "you are no bother. We just want you well and strong again. You could never be a bother to anyone."

Shalagh fluffed up Tara's pillow. Rylie crawled upon the bunk and laid her tiny hand on Tara's forehead.

"I think her head feels cooler," surmised Rylie staring into Tara's face. "I'll stay with you if you want me to," she offered. "Are you lonesome?"

"No, that's all right," replied Tara smiling weakly. "I'll only fall asleep anyway. Thank you Rylie, but I am much too tired to be lonesome."

They waited only minutes until Tara drifted off again. Leaving the stateroom and entering the dining area, they were greeted by Mr. Lee. "You girls want to join Mr. Lee up on deck?" he invited. "It is milking time for Pitty and Patty."

Rylie nodded her head and reached for Shalagh's hand.

"We'll have to get some jackets," remarked Shalagh.

"No, no need," explained Mr. Lee, "there are slickers hanging in the passageway."

They donned heavy slickers with hoods and made their way to the deck above.

"Wait here," instructed Mr. Lee upon reaching the deck.

He disappeared through another passage leaving them momentarily alone. It was then that Shalagh realized they were moving at a good clip with sails unfurled and filled with the wind. It was a beautiful sight to behold. Mr. Lee soon reappeared with Pitty and Patty the goats. Rylie took to them, immediately.

"Don't they get cold out her on deck?" she asked Mr. Lee as she patted their noses cautiously.

"Oh, they don't stay out here," Mr. Lee assured her. "They have own room, like stable. Chickens live there too," he explained. "I show you someday, ok?"

"How long ago did we leave Londonderry, Mr. Lee?" questioned Shalagh looking out across the gray rolling water. She could see land in the distance on either side.

"Before dinner time," stated Mr. Lee who was now seated on a little three legged stool milking Patty the goat, "wind switched, we go. Should clear Lake Foyle and be in North Channel by nightfall, if wind keep up."

"Are we headed then for Canada?" asked Shalagh.

"After we stop at Liverpool for Cargo," said Mr. Lee. "We flying empty now. We take on a full load and then we be on our way. Say, Missy," he continued, "there were a couple of men asking about a little girl. I rode in with the Captain for some supplies not too long before we left and they were asking him had he taken on any passengers."

"What did the Captain say?" queried Shalagh as she attempted to conceal the feeling of panic that suddenly engulfed her.

"Captain, he say it not his policy to take on passengers, especially children," said Mr. Lee. "They tell him what little girl look like, but Captain say he never saw her and bid them good day."

"What did they look like, Mr. Lee?" questioned Shalagh softly.

" Mean! Mr. Lee didn't like them. Little girl be safe as long as she on this ship," declared Mr. Lee. "We sail far, far away from them pretty quick."

No more was spoken about the subject and Mr. Lee finished milking the goats and returned them to their stable. Shalagh and Rylie waited on deck for his return. Shalagh watched the distant shore with quiet reverence realizing it was probably the last time she would ever see her beloved Ireland again. If it were possible she would stay and endeavor to find Caleb and Dylan, but she must take Tara and Rylie to a better place. Her thoughts were interrupted by Mr. Lee's return. Rylie eagerly helped Mr. Lee carry the milk to the galley below. She had not heard the conversation between Shalagh and Mr. Lee. She had been too absorbed in caring for the goats.

"If wind keep up, we be in Liverpool pretty fast," commented Mr. Lee as he strained and poured the milk into a container and placed it where it would keep cool.

The Christiana arrived in the harbor at Liverpool on a morning fresh with the smell of spring. The air felt warm on their faces as Shalagh and Rylie took to the deck watching the scenery as they came into port. In the days that had ensued Annabelle's concern had grown for Tara. Her condition hadn't become any worse, but neither did she seem improved. As soon as the anchor was dropped in the harbor, a dispatch was sent and a physician soon arrived to attend Tara. Shalagh waited nervously in the dining salon while Annabelle went with the doctor to Tara's room.

Surprisingly his prognosis was greatly encouraging. The doctor determined that Tara's condition was treatable with much rest and proper attention. He felt the ocean voyage would be excellent for her. She was to have nutritious food and when she gained more strength she would be allowed to lounge on the deck in the warm sun. He gave Annabelle complete instructions on Tara's care. Annabelle took to the task of caring for Tara with a fervent endeavor.

It took the most part of a week to take on cargo and the weather became more and more warmed by spring breezes. On the sixth day in port, Annabelle suggested that Shalagh and Rylie accompany her to Liverpool where she needed to take care of some business. Shalagh was somewhat concerned about taking Rylie away from the protection of the ship. Still it would be interesting to see Liverpool and she also needed to make purchases for herself, Tara and Rylie. She found that someone had made ample provision for them to do so. The bag with the boarding passes had also contained sufficient monies for their needs.

They accompanied Annabelle to several places of business, but when it became apparent that business would keep her occupied for most of the afternoon, Annabell suggested that the girls shop alone and then meet her at a designated spot later in the afternoon. They could then have dinner and return to the Christiana together.

Shalagh and Rylie browsed through the shops, trying on and finally purchasing enough apparel to last for sometime. They shopped in the vicinity where Annabelle planned to meet them later. Their mood had been pleasant and light-hearted but after leaving a small dress shop Shalagh was suddenly overwhelmed by a great sense of uneasiness. She attempted to shrug it off but her fears only seem to grow.

"Rylie, I think we will end our shopping and join Annabelle now," stated Shalagh as she nervously looked behind her.

"That's all right, I'm kind of tired anyway," replied Rylie. She was hugging a doll that Shalagh had purchased for her. "I want to show Tara my doll," she smiled hapily.

Their purchases were being sent to the ship so they carried no packages other than the doll. With a sense of urgency now, Shalagh desired to find the shortest way back to the location where they had left Annabelle. She turned around quickl;y holding tightly to Rylie's tiny hand. She nearly collided with a gentleman who had been walking behind them. Not stopping for apologizes she hurried down the street. She sensed someone was following them and tried to make haste to reach their appointed rendezvous with Annabelle. At the street corner a hack pulled up blocking their way.

"Want a ride, ladies?" called down the driver.

"No, no, thank you," Shalagh answered him curtly as she tried to push her way past the carriage. The driver sat on a high seat in front and outside of the cab. "Be happy to take you anywhere you want to go," yelled the driver insistently.

"No, we don't care for a ride," retorted Shalagh. She was trying to see the building where they had left Annabelle, but the hack obscured her view.

The windows of the cab were covered with dark curtains drawn across the glass. Still Shalagh could distinguish a shadowy form of a figure seated inside the coach. A movement inside the cab caught her attention and made her heart pound wildly. Then someone pulled back the curtain from the window and a face that Shalagh would never forget stared out from the cab with dark penetrating eyes. The face was thin and gaunt, terribly scared and framed with black, straight hair, which fell unevenly onto the shoulders. But it was his eyes that terrified her. They were filled with evil as his menacing stare held her frozen to the spot in fear. Slowly, the door of the hack began to open. Shalagh could not move. A cane thrust forward and its curved handle nearly caught Rylie by the waist. A heavy hand came down on Shalagh's shoulder.

"Shopping all done, girls?" thundered Annabelle's voice as she quickly steered both girls down the street away from the hack. She stared back as the driver spurred away in great haste.

"What was going on there?" questioned Annabelle as she hurried them along.

"We…we don't know," stammered Shalagh. "They wanted to give us a ride, but the occupant was frightening."

"Yes," agreed Rylie who had remained completely still during the encounter but shaken. "I want to go back to the ship."

"I think that would be best," insisted Annabelle. "It's a good thing my business finished early and I came looking for you two. Hard telling what would have happened had I not come along.

By the time they had arrived back at the Christiana the two

girls had calmed down. Annabelle had surely rescued them. As they sat down to dinner in the comfortable safety of the ship, Shalagh felt as though they had found a home and a true friend in Annabelle.

Chapter Fourteen

Shalagh adored the Christiana. They had been at sea now for nearly a week. She stood at the deck rail enjoying every moment of this lovely day. The morning was beautiful with a brisk breeze blowing and the Christiana was moving fast with full canvas unfurled. The sky was a vivid blue dotted with tiny white clouds. All about them was the glistening blue-green water capped with cresting white waves. The air was warm and fresh. Shalagh threw back her head and let the wind and sun caress her face and filter through her long dark hair.

"It is lovely, isn't it," observed Tara who was lounging in a chair close bye.

"Aye, it is like a fresh breath of life," agreed Shalagh. "I think I could live on this ship forever."

"I love it too," said Tara as she sat with her eyes closed, taking in the warm sun.

Rylie had gone to help Mr. Lee with his chores in what he called the stable.

"Yes," said Shalagh, "If only we could find Caleb and Dylan, I believe I could almost find some real peace in my life."

"We will find them, won't we?" questioned Tara opening her eyes and looking intently at Shalagh.

"We will not stop until we do," Shalagh assured her. "I

149

believe we will all be together soon. I miss them so, Caleb with his strength and Dylan so quick to bring joy to your heart.

"Wouldn't it be wonderful if they were waiting for us in Canada?" smiled Tara.

"They might well be," stated Shalagh. "Sometimes I wonder if they might be on this very ship. There are many men and older boys working aboard and we haven't seen them close up."

"No, it's like a ship divided," said Tara. "The sailors are not allowed on our deck and we are not allowed over there. Do you really think the boys might be on the Christiana?" excitedly questioned Tara.

"It is just a thought," replied Shalagh, "but, I can't help but wonder."

"I'll have to watch more closely when I'm out here on deck. There were a couple of attractive appearing young sailors working on deck yesterday, but it wasn't our brothers," stated Tara with a sigh.

"Tara Frizzle, you better not let Annabelle hear you admiring the young men on the opposite deck," scolded Shalagh good-naturedly. "She will lock us up below."

"Yes, she would probably put blinders on me," laughed Tara, "although I wasn't admiring them, I was only observing."

"Somebody going blind?" asked Annabelle stepping up on deck behind the girls.

"No, laughed Shalagh," with a wink at Tara. "It's just that the sun is really bright today."

"It is that and you've had enough sun, young lady. Best go below and put some cream on your face. You look a bit burned to me," said Annabelle in a motherly tone.

"All right, I think I've had enough sun," agreed Tara while gathering up a blanket she had draped over her lap. "I'll see you below."

Annabelle walked over to where Shalagh stood and took hold of the deck rail with her strong hands and stared out over the rolling water. The wind touched her face and blew little wisps of hair about her temples. It was predominantly gray and held back from her face in a tight bun.

"I was pretty once, like you girls," Annabelle reminisced while staring at the sea. "You'd never think so now," she declared turning to face Shalagh.

"I think you are very attractive," Shalagh honestly assured her.

"Nah, my skin looks and feels like tough leather from my many years at sea. That's why I don't want Tara to ruin her pretty Irish complexion," voiced Annabelle. "The sea's hard on you. I really wanted to talk to you alone," explained Annabelle changing the subject, "without Rylie and Tara around."

"Something wrong?" questioned Shalagh.

"No, no, but, I've been wanting to talk to you ever since we left Liverpool," answered Annabelle. "Just never seemed the right time. You girls didn't know but we had callers after we returned to the ship from that incident in Liverpool. A couple of men came right on deck and insisted that we had a little girl by the name of Rylie Frizzle on board. They had papers to take her with them. They told the Captain that her Uncle was searching for her and that there was a ransom to be paid if she were found."

"Why didn't they find her?" asked Shalagh, fear rising in her voice.

"We didn't let them any where near that child," reported Annabelle. "She has been through enough. They demanded to see our passenger list. Captain said we didn't have one. This is not a passenger ship. We deal in cargo only he told them. Yes it would seem they followed us right to the ship after we left them in Liverpool. We pulled out into the harbor early."

"Was one of them that horrible looking man?" asked Shalagh.

"No, neither of them looked like the man you described," commented Annabelle.

"I hope we haven't caused any trouble for you and the Captain," Shalagh offered with sincere regret.

She had only seen the Captain a couple of times in the dining area. He usually took his meals in the Pilothouse. He appeared austere and paid no attention to the girls whatsoever. Shalagh felt the Captain was not one you would want to anger.

"Ain't causing us no trouble," declared Annabelle. "But, what in the world do they want with poor little Rylie? If this uncle cared for her so much, how'd she come to be in such a bad way?" asked Annabelle.

"As far as I know, there is no uncle," related Shalagh. "My uncle supposedly died, so I'm confused as to whom this person might be."

"Poor little Rylie," said Annabelle, "someone is certainly after her, that's for sure."

"Yes, it could be they are after her fortune. Rylie could be quite wealthy," explained Shalagh. "Her father who is my father's brother owned the linen mills in Londonderry. He was killed in an accident at the mills. The rest of her family was left to die of starvation and improper care. Rylies mother died in prison and her brother in the workhouse. My own dear family has suffered terrible heartache and tragedy and our brothers have mysteriously disappeared.

"Oh child, this is all too horrible," Annabelle despaired. "We thought it was the famine from which you escaped, but it seems there is much more that has driven you from Ireland," she sighed shaking her head in disbelief.

The conversation was interrupted abruptly by Mr. Lee and Rylie.

"Mr. Lee let me milk Pitty and Patty," said the happy child gleefully. "They didn't even care, they liked me."

"She do good job," announced Mr. Lee. "Me think me maybe hire Rylie to help with chores."

Mr. Lee and Rylie hurried off with their pail of milk chattering happily away together.

"Shalagh, I must get back to work," informed Annabelle laying a rough hand on Shalagh's arm. But you girls are safe as long as you are on board the Christiana. So try not to worry," she smiled reassuringly.

"Thank you," Annabelle smiled Shalagh. "Annabelle, is that a ship some distance ahead of us," inquired Shalagh pointing off toward the horizon.

"Yes, it's loaded with refuges bound for Canada. There's two of them out there. Coffin ships we call them, overloaded and in bad shape to begin with," sniffed Annabelle in disgust.

"I wasn't sure, it's so far away," surveyed Shalagh staring hard into the distance. I noticed it yesterday too."

"I hope your brothers aren't on one of those ships," Annabelle said shaking her head.

"You don't think they could be working aboard this ship, do you?" Shalagh questioned Annabelle, turning to look straight at her now.

"No, dearie, not unless they are going by some other name, and then I would have not way of telling," she disclosed. "What do they look like?"

"Well Caleb is seventeen, tall, muscular and he has blond hair and a serious nature. Dylan is only thirteen with dark hair and the sweetest face and he makes you laugh," described Shalagh.

"We have no one that young working aboard ship," Annabelle assured her. "I am really sorry, but they are not traveling with us."

"Thank you, Annabelle," said Shalagh. "She felt Annabelle was sincere in telling her the truth.

After Annabelle left, Shalagh continued to watch the ship far off on the horizon. It was so tiny, sometimes disappearing completely and then reappearing as a speck again. Shalagh then bowed her head and prayed.

"Dear God, please take care of Caleb and Dylan, wherever they may be and let no harm or injury befall them. Thank you for the safety of this ship and for your protection over us."

Soon days turned into weeks as time flew by. Shalagh was given a freedom she had not known since the death of her beloved parents. Tara and Rylie were so well cared for by Annabelle and Mr. Lee that it gave her time to rest or read or just walk on the deck. She could do whatever she liked. It gave her much time to think about the future and what they would do upon their arrival in Canada. She had no idea. Caleb and Dylan could be waiting for them, but if not, where would they go she pondered.

The weather had remained pleasant with only a few sudden squalls until the fourth week into the journey. Now the sky had turned an ominous color of yellow and the wind had picked up to gale force. The sails were lowered and secured and the Christiana made tight.

"You girls stay below," Annabelle warned during breakfast. "No walking on deck today. This thing might just blow over, but Captain doesn't like the look of it. He thinks we are in for some rough weather."

The girls spent the morning in the parlor attempting to sew and read, but the rolling and pitching of the ship made it impossible to concentrate. The storm became more violent and dark clouds covered the sky causing an eerie blackness to prevail. Shalagh had never heard the wind howl with such fierceness. Lightning opened up the clouds again and again followed by loud crashes and booms of thunder. There was no preparation of the noon meal. The girls finally staggered to the security of their cabin. The Christiana rolled with the waves and then suddenly she dropped between the crests of two waves. She arose abruptly throwing everyone and everything not fastened down wildly about. There came a deafening crash and the sound of splintering timber. The Christiana groaned and shook violently then followed an eerie silence.

"I think we're split in to," said Tara with a quivering voice and a look of shock on her face.

The girls waited, to afraid to move. Then the sound of Annabelle's husky voice suddenly revitalized them.'

"Girls, girls," she shouted, "are you all right in there?" she yelled as she pounded on the cabin door.

"Yes, I think we are," returned Shalagh as she made her way to the door and pulled it open revealing a corridor littered with debris. A large whole was visible through the ceiling above.

"We have lost a mast and some of our men were hurt when the rigging came down. Sure you're all right though?" she yelled again over the roaring of the storm.

"Yes, were shaken up a bit, but we're fine," the girls assured her as they peered nervously into the hole through the ceiling. Rain was now pouring through the opening into the corridor.

"I don't think we're in any real danger," disclosed Annabelle, "and it looks like the worst of whatever hit us is over. I've got to get back up on deck and help. Glad you girls are okay."

The girls made their way through the water and debris to the dining salon where Mr. Lee was scurrying about attempting to put things back in place.

"Everyone fine?" questioned Mr. Lee.

"Just shook up a bit," stated Tara.

"I would be all right," said Rylie, "except I'm very hungry."

"Rylie, you never cease to amaze me with that appetite or yours," said Shalalgh.

"You sit down and hold tight to table and Mr. Lee find you some food. Can't have Rylie hunger," he declared humorously.

"Tara, if you and Rylie want to stay here, I think I will go above and see if I can help," stated Shalagh.

"I don't know," said Tara. "Annabelle may not welcome the idea."

"Well, then she can send be back," said Shalagh determined to go on deck and help.

Quickly she made her way through the passage picking up and donning an oil skin on her way through. Once on deck she witnessed with mixed emotions the devastation to the ship created by the storm. She was overjoyed that the Christiana remained afloat and had not floundered and sank into the watery depths of the ocean. But, on the other hand there was great destruction and the ship was in a state of chaos. Part of the main mast had fallen across the deck, causing canvas and lines to fall in a tangled mess everywhere. Shalagh stepped over some of the downed rigging. The wind was still blowing strong, but the worst of the storm had rolled away and blue sky was showing in the distance. The ship was awash with water from huge waves that had pummeled the ship.

Annabelle was shouting instructions to sailors who were frantically at work on the mid and forward sections, trying to assess the damage. Annabelle stopped and knelt down beside a fallen deck hand. He had been injured and was entangled in the wreckage. She spoke to him for a minute and then bowed her head and began to pray. One after another, the men scurrying about realized Annabelle was praying and the sound of husky men's voices became still across the ship and the wind seemed to increase the volume of Annabelle's gritty voice amid the hush of other voices. Powerful, brawny men stood silently as Annabelle prayed.

"Dear God, dear God," were the first words that reverberated across the deck and caught the men's attention. "Dear God, thank you," Annabelle roared over the sound of the wind. "Thank you, that not one person on this ship was killed by that murderous storm. Not one... I said, not one, Lord. We're going to take this ship and every person on it safely to port. Your Holy Word tells us that no weapon formed against us shall prosper and we've had a weapon formed but, it ain't going to prosper. Now Lord, Lem here needs help and Barney over there needs your touch too. I can fix them up pretty good, but you take it from there and do the rest if there's more that needs to be taken care of. Thank you, most merciful father—thank you so much."

Annabelle raised her self up and took notice of the men standing in silence around her. She did not see Shalagh, who was behind her near the coach house.

"All right, mates," Annabelle said in a more gentle tone, "some of you help get these men below and the rest of you return to work."

Believing that she was only in the way, Shalagh decided to go below, but before she could move she became paralyzed by the spectacle looming up before her eyes. She stared with disbelief, stunned and unable to move or speak. A ship in full sail was bearing down upon them by the bow and fast. The canvas was ripped and shredded and the hemp shrouds were slack and snapping in the wind. She came on fast lighting the remaining dark clouds with a pulsating red glow. Flames and fire had engulfed her midsection and were swiftly climbing up her rigging. Someone let out a yell and all eyes turned to see the approaching ship. Like a streak of lightning she came up on the port side and for a moment it appeared she would slide on by with inches to spare. All at once she scraped with a groan and slammed screaming like a banshee along the port side of the Chriatiana. For a moment the two ships were locked together at the midsection, then with a shudder that rocked booth ships like an explosion the phantom ship lurched forward and shrieked on past, picking up tremendous speed as she pulled away. There was no discernible life on board and the helm not yet consumed with fire, spun wildly on it's own with no visible hands to guide it. No one moved or spoke aboard the Christian until Annabelle's voice screamed,

"Dear God, help us! Where did that thing come from?" Then she yelled at the deck hands, "Assess the port side and planking. Check everything for fire," she roared like a bullhorn.

Sailors scrambled with capable dexterity in the rigging above and on deck they feverishly began to untangle the mass of broken lines. They shouted back and forth as they worked. Shalagh stood in absolute bewilderment. A slack line went whizzing by her head, barely missing her. Realizing she was only in the way and undoubtedly in danger herself, Shalagh made her way back to the dining salon. Tara and Rylie were eagerly awaiting her return.

"Are we going to sink?" asked Rylie all wide eyed and frightened.

"We are still afloat," Shalagh assured them.

"What was all that noise a few minutes ago," questioned Tara. "It sounded like a woman screaming."

"We thought the side of the ship was coming off," whimpered Rylie. "I hope Pitty and Patty are safe."

"Well the storm did a lot of damage to the sale and rigging, and then we were slammed into by a runaway vessel. That's what made the screaming noise. I don't know how much damage we have sustained," related Shalagh.

"Oh, do you think we should go topside in case we need to take to the lifeboats?" asked Tara.

"No Annabelle has everything under control and she will come and tell us if that is necessary," Shalagh assured them.

"Another ship hit us?" questioned Tara now coming to a full realization of what Shalagh had just told them.

"It was more that it scraped our side, but it was frightening. I stood there speechless, afraid to move," related Shalagh. "I still can hardly believe what I witnessed. It was a fearful sight."

"Was it a ghost ship?" asked Rylie with a look of fear in her eyes. She had been listening to Clancy and Swede's tall stories of the high seas.

Just then Annabelle's booming voice resounded from the companionway.

"You girls come on up here. The storm is almost blown away," she shouted loudly.

The girls scurried to the deck above anxious to see what Annabelle wanted. The sun was brightly shining and although the sky behind them was black, huge puffy white clouds and blue sky was now over the Christiana. Men were still frantically working to clear the deck of debris and restore the mast to some degree of workability. The mysterious phantom ship that had struck them was no where to be seen.

"Are you girls all in one piece?" questioned Annabelle while mopping her forehead with the back of her hand and looking a bit weary.

"Yes, yes, we are," they all assured her in unison.

"It was a bad one," said Annabelle, "the storm I mean. We get a lot of them, but this one was an unusually wild one. Short lived, but mean as the devil himself.

"Is everyone else all right," quizzed Tara.

"We had a couple of sailors hurt, but they'll be fine. We're putting into port in a few more days and a real doctor can then look at them. That is if we can fix the mast and rigging," explained Annabelle.

"Are we near Canada?" questioned Tara enthusiastically feeling a wave of excitement at the thought of coming into port.

"We're close and if it hadn't been for that storm we may have sighted land in a couple of days," stated Annabelle. "It will take a bit longer now."

The air had abruptly changed after the storm, from warm and humid to suddenly cool. Rylie stood shivering as she listened to Annabelle and watched the men at work.

"You girls best get below, now," suggested Annabelle. "It has turned much cooler. Follow me and I will take you through the companionway to the dining salon. Men are working to repair some damage near your cabin right now."

"Was there much damage done to the Christiana by the ship that struck us?" questioned Shalagh.

"How'd you know about that?" asked Annabelle with a puzzling look on her face.

"I—well, I came up on deck to see how much damage the storm had done and I saw the ship strike us," explained Shalagh rather sheepishly.

"Well, it seems not," declared Annabelle, "but we can better assess our damages when we reach port. God sure had his protecting hand upon us. It's a miracle that ship didn't do us great harm.

"Is there any hope that help might reach the ship that grazed us?" asked Shalagh.

"Hope for that vessel must have vanished sometime ago. She's a lost soul, flying before the wind, bound for nowhere," Annabelle agonized.

Annabelle said no more and soon left them safe in the dining salon where they stayed quite comfortable amid the noise of sawing, hammering and shouting voices. Sometime later, Mr. Lee brought the girls a tray of food that he had managed to salvage from the overturned boxes and cans in the pantry.

"Much work to be done in pantry," he told them.

"We could help you," offered Tara.

"No, me do. Me only one knows where things belong. Thank you much, though Missy," said Mr. Lee with his continuous smile showing on his face.

Chapter Fifteen

Early on the morning of June 30, 1847, land was sighted from the Christiana. Hardly visible at first it seemed to appear and then disappear with the up and down motion of the ship. Finally, land could clearly be distinguished. The sight was extremely glorious after their long voyage. Annabelle called the girls on deck and soon Mr. Lee and Clancy joined them. It was a time of great rejoicing. Annabelle informed the girls that if it had not been dark and foggy, they would have sighted land sooner as they had passed through the straits of Belle Isle the night before.

"After we round the Gaspe Peninsula we'll then enter the St. Lawrence," explained Annabelle with a happy sound to her voice. She was much relieved to be home.

"How long before we reach our destination," inquired Shalagh eagerly, as they peered from the deck and watched the land of the distant shoreline pass before by them.

"We've still a ways to go, but the worse part of the journey is over," announced Annabelle. "We've come nearly 2000 miles since leaving Liverpool. Now if we can sail this old girl up the river to Quebec, that will be a mighty big relief," sighed Annabelle.

Annabelle soon hurried off to give orders to a couple of

sailors on the forward deck. The girls continued to watch the scenery awed by the appearance of the land. Finally, the sound of the breakfast bell called them below.

Their voyage at sea had done wonders for Tara. Under the watchful care of Annabelle, both Tara and Rylie had been returned to good health. However, Shalagh was a little concerned about Rylie today. She was cross at breakfast and ate very little, both behaviors unusual for Rylie. She declined Mr. Lee's invitation to help with chores and when Shalagh asked her why, she just pouted and said nothing. Shalagh dismissed Rylie's behavior to excitement over their arrival in Canada. After Breakfast the girls went back on deck to enjoy the view once more.

"What is wrong Rylie?" questioned Shalagh. "Are you unhappy about something?"

Rylie's mood had become extremely cross and restless.

"No", answered Rylie lowering her head and whimpering as she spoke.

"Then why are you crying?" demanded Tara putting her arm lovingly around the little girl. "Her face is hot," disclosed Tara placing her hand on Rylie's cheek. "Are you sick Rylie? Do you have pain anywhere?"

"Rylie, honey," insisted Shalagh, "why didn't you let us know that you did not feel well?" "Let's take her to the parlor and I will find Annabelle".

The girls quickly took Rylie to the parlor. Shalagh returned a short time later with Annabelle right behind her. After a quick observation, Annabelle suggested that the child be taken to the girls' stateroom. Rylie was very ill throughout the day. She could keep nothing on her stomach and she restlessly rolled about in her bed, finding no comfort from her illness.

"What do you think is wrong with her?" implored both Shalagh and Tara of Annabelle.

"She has been so well throughout the trip," remarked Shalagh.

"I can't be positive what it is," commented Annabelle, "but I am inclined to think it is just something that will quickly pass. We will pray to our Father in Heaven. He knows all and he is good medicine."

After saying that Annabelle and the girls bowed in quiet prayer while Mr. Lee stood in the hallway, just outside the stateroom door repeating Amen, Amen, Amen, Amen in a continuous droning sound while they prayed together.

Shalagh and Tara remained watchful with Rylie through the day and most of the night. Annabelle and Mr. Lee came frequently to help them tend to Rylie. Before morning the fever broke and Rylie fell into a deep exhaustive sleep. Shalagh and Tara weary from caring for the sick child fell asleep with her. They both woke to Annabelle's soft rap on the door. Annabelle opened the door carefully so as not to awake the sleeping child entrusted to her care.

"Is Rylie still sleeping?" whispered Annabelle gruffly.

"Yes," returned Tara in a soft whisper.

Annabelle motioned for the girls to follow her into the passageway as she tip toed out the door. The girls were fully dressed having been so tired they had not changed from their daytime attire.

"How is she?" quizzed Annabelle.

"She appears to be sleeping well with no more fever or upset stomach," disclosed Shalagh with relief.

"Good, I thought she looked better every time I entered the room. Poor little tyke, must have been something she ate," suggested Annabelle. Then looking at Shalagh and Tara she asked with evident sincerity, "You girls feeling all right?"

"We are fine," Tara assured her. "Just a little tired after last night. Rylie was really sick."

"I know," replied Annabelle. "Why don't you girls go and see if Mr. Lee will rustle you up some breakfast. I'll sit with the child for awhile. We're at anchor anyways, waiting for the inspectors to allow us to pass Gross Isle.

"Gross Isle," responded Tara, "what is that?"

"Ships have to pass medical inspection before they can go any farther up the St. Lawrence," explained Annabelle. "There's a lot of sickness and fever coming in these refugee ships. Shouldn't be any trouble for us though, since we don't usually carry any passengers. I think they'll just let us pass."

"You don't think they will stop us because of Rylie's sickness, do you?" questioned Shalagh.

"Sure hope not but wouldn't hurt none to pray about it though," stated Annabelle after giving some thought to Shalagh's question.

Mr. Lee was happy to prepare something for the two girls to eat.

"How's little Miss Rylie," inquired Mr. Lee without his usual smile.

"She is greatly improved," revealed Tara, "we think she is all right now. Annabelle is sitting with her."

"Oh, so happy to hear," responded Mr. Lee as his countenance brightened with a big smile. "It would not be good if they quarantined us."

"Why would they do that?" questioned Shalagh.

"Oh, missy, ships all around us with many sick people. Too many sick—ships must stay here in quarantine," he explained.

"You mean they could keep us here and not even let us off the ship?" asked Tara in dismay.

"Might be, we wait see. Inspector on board now," stated Mr. Lee. "He look at everyone before he go."

Even before they finished eating, Shalagh and Tara were summoned to the parlor.

The inspector was waiting for them. He was an older man with thinning hair and wearing thick glasses. He asked a few questions about their health in general. He looked down their throats and checked their eyes with a strange looking instrument.

"Uh huh, yes," he kept repeating and finally, "yes, yes, you both appear to be in good health," he concluded as he reached for his small black bag he had placed on the table and abruptly left the parlor.

It wasn't until just before dark set in that Annabelle came to tell them what the inspector had decided. Rylie was so much recovered that Mr. Lee had encouraged them to bring her to the dining salon for some warm broth. She was happily chattering away with the girls and Mr. Lee when Annabelle found them.

"Well, you sure look better," stated Annabelle with a big grin. "Feeling good again, Honey?" she asked Rylie putting her hand to Rylies' forehead.

"I'm all better," Rylie assured them, "and tomorrow I can help Mr. Lee again"

"We don't want to rush it," voiced Annabelle, "let's see how you feel in the morning, honey."

"All right," agreed Rylie once again her sweet self.

"I want to tell you girls and Mr. Lee that the inspector cleared us to travel inland to Montreal. We are under a partial quarantine, though. When we arrive in Montreal they will probably lift it," Annabelle explained.

"What is a partial quarantine?" questioned Shalagh.

"It means we must remain in Montreal where we will make repairs anyways. Also, no one can leave the ship until the quarantine is fully lifted," stated Annabelle.

"How are they going to make repairs to the ship if we are quarantined?" asked Mr. Lee.

"Well, the authorities will have to let us do something about that. We're taking in water and we are loaded with cargo," stated Annabelle. "We sure don't want to lose it."

After much discussion and answering of questions, Rylie was finally tucked into bed for the night. Shalagh and Tara went up on deck before retiring. It was a warm July night. The sky was dotted with a myriad of bright stars and the moon shown brightly, illuminating the many ships at anchor around them.

"It all appears so peaceful and serene," declared Tara. "You would not know that these ships are filled with the sick and dying."

"Yes, but it is true, according to what Annabelle has told us," acknowledged Shalagh with remorse.

"My, but it is warm, with no breeze at all," said Shalagh, wiping her forehead. "Perhaps we should sleep on deck."

"I think we will find it more comfortable below," suggested Shalagh. "Besides, Annabelle seems to feel we are in danger of illness just from the air itself. She is not happy about our position so close to what she calls the 'coffin ships'."

"It doesn't look peaceful anymore," said Tara with a sudden shiver. "We have too many memories of death and sickness. Let us go below," she suggested sadly.

Rylie was sleeping undisturbed when they returned to the cabin and in spite of everything Shalagh and Tara soon drifted off to a peaceful night of rest.

Chapter Sixteen

The Christiana limped into the harbor of Montreal nearly two weeks later under great duress. She could go no farther without repairs. Even here, ships were moored all around them with the sick and dying. Distance had not caused them to escape the coffin ships. The stench of death and sickness was everywhere. The partial quarantine remained in effect but the Christiana was allowed to move out and away from the other ships to berth at a nearby shipyard. She was taking on water and it was feared she might be a hazard to the harbor. After a day and a half the crew was allowed to remove the cargo from the hold onto the dock below. From there the cargo was taken and stored in a large warehouse nearby. This enabled them to save the cargo and lessen the danger of sinking until the repairs could be made. This took several days to accomplish. No one but the crew was permitted on the dock and they were not allowed to leave the area. The Christiana was under constant surveillance. The captain was given permission to remove the two injured sailors to a small hospital on the outskirts of Montreal to receive medical attention.

On the fourth day in port, Shalagh and Tara sat on deck taking in busy scene of men hard at work. Rylie was helping Mr. Lee in the pantry. Clancy was helping hoist the large crates from the cargo hold onto the deck. From there the crates were lowered over the side of the Christiana on the dock below. The crates were then removed to a storehouse only a few feet away from the dock. Suddenly two men approached Clancy.

"Where could we find the Captain," solicited one of the men.

"Watch your heads, there's a crate coming up from the hold!" shouted Clancy at the startled men.

The two men ducked just in time to avoid a near collision.

"Keep bringing up those crates!" yelled Clancy at one of the deck hands. "I'll be right back. Come on, I'll show you to the Captain," said Clancy motioning to the men to follow him.

"Probably more doctors," offered Tara.

"It would be good if they would lift the quarantine. There is no sickness of any kind on board," declared Shalagh. "At least then we might be permitted to go into Montreal."

"Just to walk to dry land again would be a joy," laughed Tara. "Still, I do love the Christiana."

The girls were seated on chairs lined against the pilot house and the men had come along on the opposite side, unaware of their presents. The sun was warm and the girls lay back in the chairs soaking in its warm rays. Suddenly Tara sat up straight in her chair turning her head and looking toward the main deck a few steps below.

"What was that?" asked Tara.

"I didn't hear anything," stated Shalagh noting her sisters' apparent alarm.

"Psst, Psst, girls," Annabell's voice softly beckoned in a hoarse whisper from her position on the steps beside the pilot house.

This time both Tara and Shalagh heard the sound and jumped to their feet.

"What is it?" asked Tara who was nearest and first to reach the steps leading to the main deck.

"There aint't no time to explain," panted Annabelle nearly out of breath. "Hurry, girls follow me," she ordered.

They followed her obediently as far as the main hatch. Here, Annabelle stopped in front of a large wooden box.

"There's trouble brewing. Girls you will have to leave now. Don't give me any argument 'lessen you want to end up in jail. Two men just came aboard and they have a paper which says they are to take Rylie back to Ireland and you girls to jail. The only way of escape is for you both to climb into this shipping case quickly now. Help them Clancy," she commanded as Clancy joined them.

"But, what about Rylie?" questioned Shalagh while obliging Annabelle by climbing into the box with Clancy's help and sliding down to the bottom of their rather small confining quarters.

"Don't worry about her," declared Annabelle, "I took care of it. Just be very still. Don't move until you're told to," she cautioned as she hurried away.

Immediately Clancy clamped down the lid making it pitch dark inside. It was stuffy and they had little room in which to move, but air came through several small holes cut into the side of the crates. Soon the approaching sound of footsteps could be heard. The girls remained very still. Shalagh could see somewhat through the small hole on her side but her view was very limited. Captain Logans' voice was now distinguishable very close to the girls confined space in the crate.

"Yes, that may all be true," commented the Captain in his rough seaman's voice. "But as you can see, we have no record of any such person on board this ship. Our records list all of the crew and help. We are not a passenger ship and we list no passengers.

"But this is where there seems to be some sort of error," remarked one of the men. "Our investigation has produced not one but two doctors who claim they have been aboard the Christiana and witnessed the presence of a small female child and two nearly adult girls. Now, did they only imagine what they say?" he retorted in a sharp tone.

"No," said Captain Logan, "I am sure the good doctors did witness the people that you speak of, but we have so many ships about us with so many sick, the good doctors could have easily been confused as to which ship they saw girls."

"Let me tell you Captain," now spoke the other gentleman in anger. "We are going to search every inch of this ship until we find them."

"Rylies' dear Uncle Rutgers would be here himself, but he is deathly afraid of ships and water and we are committed to returning that poor child back into his tender care," stated the second man more calmly.

"Yes, as for those despicable girls who kidnapped the child from her grieving uncle, they will be found, put into prison and punished severely!" announced the first man shouting across the deck.

Captain," interrupted Clancy, "we need to get these crates below onto the dock. Is it all right we continue what we were doing?"

"Lower them away," ordered the Captain. "Well, gentlemen, you have searched my records and found nothing," declared Captain Logan. "Now be my guest and search about the ship until you are satisfied."

"Where do we start?" questioned one of the men who apparently knew little about ships compartments.

"Anywhere," answered the Captain. "Clancy; when you have removed these crates from the deck, please escort these gentlemen through the ship, taking them where ever they wish to go."

"Right away, Captain," obediently responded Clancy. "Come on men let's get these crates off the ship and onto the wharf."

Shalagh and Tara felt a sudden jolt as the crate in which they were confined was hoisted into the air. They remained silent, not daring to move or speak. They could hear Clancy and the deck hands yelling commands back and forth to each other, but they could see nothing now.

"Lower away, boys," commanded Clancy to someone below.

Their short journey in their temporary prison ended with a sudden thud. After that it seemed an eternity as the girls huddled together in their cramped position inside the box.

"It's getting hot in here," whispered Shalagh. "There's no air. I think they left us sitting in the hot sun. What if they forgot us?"

Just about that time they were moved again, this time there was no sound of voices. Then with a splintering sound of boards being pried loose the top of the case was opened and light pored in. The girls huddled together look up into the rough textured, but kind face of Clancy.

"Come on girls, let me give you a hand," he said as he reach strong muscular arms into the crate.

He pulled them out with little effort, one by one.

"Is it all right to speak?" asked Shalagh shaking herself and trying to get some feeling back into her limbs.

"It's all right to talk, but you've little time," he explained. "Follow me."

A horse drawn carriage soon pulled up close by them. They reached the carriage with great haste. There were no good-byes.

They were on board and moving with a fast rate of speed within minutes. The carriage held two other passengers, Rylie and Mr. Lee.

"Oh, Rylie," whispered Tara, afraid to speak out loud. "and Mr. Lee how did you get here?"

"You can talk now missies," said Mr. Lee. "Annabelle had us lowered off the stern of the boat to shore. We must move fast to keep ahead of law."

"Where are we going?" inquired Shalagh.

"We go United States," announced Mr. Lee. "Captain Logan make all plans."

"U-United States?" stuttered Tara in amazement. "I-I can't believe it."

"It be true," he assured them, "if we not caught first."

"Did the authorities see you and Rylie depart the Christiana?" questioned Shalagh.

"Have no way to know," stated Mr. Lee.

"Here Annabelle, give me this luggage to give you and a letter from Captain Logan," explained Mr. Lee, handing Shalagh the large suitcase and a letter.

Shalagh hurriedly opened the envelope containing the letter. It was brief, explaining that Mr. Lee had been given specific instructions as to where they were to be taken. A kind benefactor had made provisions for their traveling expenses and nothing more could be revealed at this time. The luggage held what belongings they had left behind in the stateroom including the envelope with money. After reading the letter she handed it to Tara.

"It doesn't say much," concluded Tara as she finished reading.

"To where in the United States are we going?" inquired Shalagh of Mr. Lee.

"We travel to city called, Detroit," said Mr. Lee softly. "Me can say no more. It is too dangerous.

Chapter Seventeen

The distance between Montreal and Detroit was a slow and arduous journey. It was a most uncomfortable, long and weary some experience. Finally, it ended on an early summer morning, the twenty-ninth day of August 1849. With jubilance and great excitement the three girls and Mr. Lee hurried from the small boat that had ferried them across the river from Canada to Detroit, on the American side.

"We are in the United States of America!" shouted Tara as soon as her feet cleared the gangplank.

"Me kiss ground," said Mr. Lee as he fell on his knees and kissed the dirt with tears streaming down his wrinkled face. "Mr. Lee make promise to my family many years ago that someday I come to America," he explained as he arose from his knees and stood with his face shining with joy.

Looking up his eyes caught sight of an American flag flying high on a building nearby. Placing his right hand across his heart he stood weeping without any show of embarrassment. He too had suffered many trials and much persecution before this day had come. As Old Glory unfurled her stars and stripes above them Shalagh, Tara and Rylie followed his example and stood in silent prayer, thanking God for his mercy and deliverance and for bringing them to this sought after land of freedom. After a few minutes Mr. Lee raised his head and opened his eyes dimmed by his tears.

They followed the line of other immigrants through immigration lines and after an hour or two of inspection and questions they were allowed to leave for their destination.

"Come girls, we go now, we need catch boat to home," stated Mr. Lee.

"We have further yet to go?" moaned Tara. "Why can't we stay her in Detroit for at least today," she pleaded.

"Some other time we come to visit, but now we must go to farm," explained Mr. Lee.

"We are going to a farm?" questioned Shalagh as she reached to pick up one of the suitcases.

Mr. Lee picked up the remaining luggage and motioned for them to follow him.

"What farm are you talking about?" yelled Shalagh trying to catch up with Mr. Lee who had taken off fast ahead of them.

"Tara, where is Rylie?" questioned Shalagh. "Oh, you have her—good. Hurry, come quickly. Do not let go of Rylies' hand or we will lose her in this crowd. Mr. Lee, wait up," called Shalagh as they made every effort to catch up with the wiry little man.

"What farm are you talking about?" demanded Shalagh, breathlessly as they met up with Mr. Lee.

"Rose Cottage Farm," said Mr. Lee as he hurried them up a gangplank unto a small sailing vessel. "Come ladies, or we miss only boat to Lexington."

"I'm tired of boats and water," whined Rylie as the craft pulled away from the pier.

"Be last time," promised Mr. Lee as he lifted Rylie upon his shoulders so she might see a better view of the shoreline.

The Sadie Jane made daily runs from Detroit to further

points north with stops all along the way. They boarded the ship at Seven A.M. and by mid morning they cleared Lake St. Clair and entered the St. Clair River. Having had no breakfast, they were delighted when a vendor made his rounds selling sandwiches and lemonade. Rylie had decided the trip was not so bad after all as she could see land on both sides once they entered the river.

The voyage up the St. Clair River was beyond imagination. It was breathtakingly beautiful. The shores on either side of the river revealed a panoramic view of green forests, pine and oak, white birch and maple. Many of the trees were already touched with brilliant tones of crimson and gold. The water was a deep azure blue which matched the sky above and everywhere white gulls circled and darted about in search of food. The suns' warm rays reflected across the ever moving deep water in a scintillating explosion of dazzling brightness. On the American side dwellings emerged here and there surrounded by abundant orchards with branches so heavy laden with fruit that they seemed to bend to kiss the ground. Cattle grazed in rich meadows. In the rushes all along the shore swam masses of swans.

"Oh my, oh my," gasped Shalagh as she stood with her hands grasping the boat rail. She stared about her with an incredulous look of unbelief. For spread out before her in all of it's splendor was the very scene she had witnessed in the dark graveyard some months ago.

"How can this be," she wept softly, "oh, how can this be?"

"What is it Shalagh, why are you crying?" comforted Tara placing her arm around her sisters waist.

"Tara, look about you," implored Shalagh. "We are witnessing a strange and wonderful scene, a mystery, a miracle, an awesome revelation.

"It is truly beautiful," agreed Tara, "but, I'm not sure what you mean."

"Tara, it is the same, the very same place the angel allowed me to see in the cemetery that terrible night in Ireland. This is the river, with its deep blue water. These are the fruit trees laden with ripe fruit and the same swans swimming by the shore," exclaimed Shalagh in sheer astonishment and excitement.

"Oh, Shalagh, yes, now I understand. It comes back to me now. It's like my dream, yes, oh how can this be?" questioned Tara in wonderment.

A village now appeared in a clearing close to the waters' edge. Women with bronze toned skin could be seen hard at work. Children with the same amazing skin color and dark hair came running to wave at them and followed the ship as far as the clearing allowed. Their happy voices floated over the water. The children appeared to be well fed, a noted contrast in comparison to the plight of Irelands' children.

"These are the children whose voices I heard but could not see. They spoke a language I could not understand. I am elated at what I see and hear, but it is more than I can comprehend. We are greatly blessed," pronounced Shalagh, unable to hold back the tears of joy.

"Yes, sister," spoke Tara, "it would appear that we have been chosen and spared by God for some purpose unknown to us."

They bowed their heads and clung to each other in tearful thanks to an every caring God. Mr. Lee stepped close beside them with Rylies' hand in his. He too gave thanks, but was unaware of what had prompted the girls to do so at this particular time. As they whispered their closing amen they opened their eyes to view an extensive lumber camp. Once again they were greeted with waving of hands and shouted loud greetings which echoed across the still primeval setting. The sound of voices reverberated into the atmosphere repeating itself until finally the sound faded away.

Rylie was captivated by the sound of repeating voices and delighted when told to return the greeting and experienced her own voice echoing across the water and into the forest.

In late afternoon the ship encountered swift currants and treacherous water at the narrow point where St. Clair River and Lake Huron meet. A strong wind was blowing out of the northeast and any attempt made to cross through the narrow stretch of water between the United States and Canada was impossible. Finally, pushed back by both their first and second attempts, the Sadie Jane put into shore on the American side.

They were most fortunate to spend the night at Fort Gratiot. Built high on the banks of the river the fort was most impressive. The buildings themselves were of white painted sidings, which stood out against the brilliant variegated green of the great pine forests beyond.

The officers and men at Fort Gratiot treated the passengers from the Sadie Jane with the greatest consideration. They spent a most comfortable night lodged at the fort. There were about fifteen sojourners in number. They all were given a filling and delicious supper in the mess hall. Afterwards, they were invited to an evening of music and the reading of poems by some of the residing soldiers. The program was most entertaining and attended by some residents of the nearby village.

After the program the girls said good night to Mr. Lee. They followed the women passengers to their assigned quarters by the light of the most spectacular moon they had ever seen. It had suddenly appeared like a huge globe of fire glowing through the dark forest on the Canadian side of the river. Gigantic in size it slowly rose higher and higher in the night sky growing less in color as it ascended. The water and land, white buildings and trees were bathed in its enhancing brightness. Many stood to watch until a most miserable insect called a mosquito sent them scurrying inside and away from the stinging bites and the maddening noise these tiny insects of torture made.

In the morning after a hearty breakfast they made sure but slow headway through the narrows into Lake Huron. As they came into the less turbulent waters of the great blue lake, they became enraptured by the view of a magnificent lighthouse on the American shore.

Late afternoon, the Sadie Jane dropped anchor below the village of Lexington in a natural harbor. From here they were taken ashore by a dinghy. Once they alighted ashore, Mr. Lee and the girls climbed a path to the top of a sandy hill. On the crest of the hill, there stood the Village of Lexington.

"You ladies stay here," instructed Mr. Lee. "You watch luggage while Mr. Lee get someone to take us to Rose Cottage Farm. Be dark soon."

He hurried off leaving the girls standing alone with the luggage.

"I'm tired," whimpered Rylie sitting down wearily on one of the cases.

Birds chirped merrily in a large tree nearby.

""It's pretty here," remarked Tara.

From where they stood the girls could see small shops lining the main street. People were busy about their business.

"I wonder how far away the farm is?" questioned Shalagh.

In a few minutes, Mr. Lee returned with a horse drawn wagon driven by a man wearing a coarse looking shirt, overalls and wearing a straw hat.

"This Mr. Billy Arnold," explained Mr. Lee. "He work at

livery. He know way to farm. Come girls, hurry, it be dark soon."

"How far do we have to travel?" inquired Shalagh in a tone evidencing her weariness from the long journey.

"It ain't far," Mr. Billy assured them. "Mile or mile an a half at most I 'spect."

Mr. Lee lifted the luggage into the wagon and helped the girls climb into a wooden seat built across the back. He then took a seat up front with Billy. It seemed Billy had never met a China man before and quickly engaged Mr. Lee in conversation about Mr. Lee himself. Apparently no one else in the village had encountered anyone from China before, either, as several people stood gaping at the wagon as it passed through the village prompting Rylie to wonder why. Billy seemed to enjoy Mr. Lee's company. Mr. Lee also seemed quite comfortable with the situation and chatted happily with Billy all the way to the farm.

"I guess, they are staring because we are new here," suggested Shalagh patting Rylies' hand.

"I think they are laughing at Mr. Lee's long hair," pouted Rylie. "I don't like them."

"They probably wish they all had hair like that," said Tara with a laugh.

The wagon headed north from the village immediately encountering thick woods on either side of the dirt trail. The trees were filled with hundreds of birds chirping their evening song. A rabbit scampered across the road in front of the wagon much to Rylies' delight. They encountered no clearing or buildings along the way, only deep woods appearing very dark and foreboding with more cheerful glimpses of the lake on occasion off to the right through the trees.

"It seems we follow the shore of the lake, I hope it isn't too far," said Shalagh. "But, wouldn't it be wonderful if Caleb and Dylan were there to greet us."

They enthusiastically all agreed.

Chapter Eighteen

Just as the last red ray's of the sun was softly fading in the sky, they arrived at the farm. The distance from Lexington to the farm was probably less than a mile. The farm was built on a large tract of cleared land on the shores of beautiful Lake Huron. Leading to the house was a long tree lined lane. As the wagon turned up the lane horses came running and whinnying from a corral near the barn. A colt frolicked in play. The house was set back some distance from the road. They came to a stop beside what appeared to be the kitchen. Perfume from a large, pink colored Rose bush hung fragrant in the cool evening breeze. In fact the whole front of the house appeared to be covered with Rose vines lavished with an abundance of roses. A stone step gave rise to a covered porch on which were placed a couple of wooden chairs and a wooden swing was suspended from the rafters of the porch roof. There was grand view of the lake and its gently flowing water not far away.

"We here girls," said Mr. Lee obviously relieved as he breathed a heavy sigh of relief. "This be Rose Cottage."

"Look, someone is home. There is a light upstairs," said Rylie pointing to a window on the second floor of the dwelling.

A light was visibly seen through an upstairs window.

Mr. Lee gently rapped on the kitchen door. After waiting a

moment and receiving no response he rapped again with more authority. Still no one came to welcome them.

"Me think light in upstairs window is reflection of sun on glass," explained Mr. Lee. "Me think no one here."

"Look, there is a small house across the road just beyond those trees," said Tara pointing in that direction. "Perhaps we should inquire over there."

Mr. Lee decided not to inquire across the street but continued to knock to see if he could get some ones attention. There was no response to their further knocking. By this time the girls had stepped up onto the porch. Rylie climbed onto the big swing with its' comfortable cushions.

"I like it here," stated Rylie with a contented smile on her face as she leaned back against the soft cushions.

"It is quite lovely," agreed Shalagh looking at the surroundings about her.

The sun had now dropped behind some low rolling hills to the west. Insects took up their night song in the soft green grass surrounding the porch.

"My orders to deliver girls safely to farm," explained Mr. Lee throwing his arms up in exasperation. "Now, what do we do?" he questioned.

"Are you sure this is the right place?" asked Tara.

"Driver say so, this Smith farm, right?" Mr. Lee questioned the driver who had been patiently waiting.

"Yep, this is the Will Smith farm all right. Both houses belong to Rose Cott5age Farm. The one across the road and this one both belong to the farm. Don't appear to be nobody at home at either place though. You all want a ride back into town?" asked the driver.

"No, we stay," said Mr. Lee as he walked over and paid the driver. "Me sure they come home soon. Thank you Mr. Billy," smiled Lee.

"Good night then," said the driver and he took off in the direction of Lexington.

"Shall we try the door?" reasoned Shalagh. "It's getting rather cool out here and it will be dark soon."

The door was not locked and they cautiously entered the kitchen. In the dim light they found a lamp on the round kitchen table and after a short search, a box of matches on the cook stove. Once the lamp was lit its light penetrated the darkness and a warm glow filled the room. It was a large country kitchen with a pantry off to the left. There was a sink with a hand pump, which produced clear cold water for which Rylie was immediately thirsty.

"I am hungry too," she gasped between gulps of water taken from the dipper held by Shalagh.

It was true they had not eaten since breakfast that morning at the fort. They were all feeling very hungry. Mr. Lee found another lamp which he lighted and was soon searching the pantry for food.

"Plenty of food here," he declared.

While the girls took one of the lamps to investigate the rest of the house, Mr. Lee brought in stacked wood from the back porch and started dinner.

The girls found the house, although much smaller than Ballymore Manor, large and spacious. The dining room off the kitchen was well furnished and comfortable. A small room off to the left of the dining area revealed a bedroom. Crossing through the dining room they entered the parlor which was massive with immense oak beams supporting the ceiling. A huge fireplace took up most of one wall, which was constructed from floor to ceiling in fieldstone. In contrast to the more masculine appearance of the ceiling and fireplace, the furniture was feminine and colorful. The couch and chairs were upholstered with fabric in patterns of roses and bright flowers of various kinds. The tables were of a rich dark gleaming wood and the floor was covered with a thick rug woven in burgundy, black, green and gray flowers. An ornate organ stood against one wall. A small library was set apart from the parlor by wooden pocket doors. The girls left a lamp lighted in the parlor and one in the dining area. They discovered a door between the dining room and kitchen which when opened revealed a dark stairway leading upstairs.

Mr. Lee was still busy in the kitchen when the girls returned. He was humming a song and briskly stirring something in a pan on the stove. He smiled nonchalantly at them.

"The sleeping area must be upstairs," suggested Shalagh apprehensively looking up the dark stairway.

"I'm sure the sleeping quarters are upstairs since the small bedroom off the dining area could not accommodate all of us," stated Tara.

"I wonder to whom this place belongs to and why we are here?" questioned Shalagh still staring up the steps that led upstairs.

"Do you really want to go up there?" questioned Tara not at all sure it was a good idea.

Mr. Lee was oblivious as to what the girls were up to. He was doing exactly what he wanted to do, cook.

"Mr. Lee," said Shalagh, "we thought we would go upstairs to see if we can find some sleeping rooms."

"That be good," agreed the little man. "You find rooms, then we eat. Little missy want food," he said winking at Rylie.

"You really don't know who owns this house?" questioned Shalagh. "And, you don't know anything more about this place or the people who own it?"

"Yes, Mr. Smith live here," answered Mr. Lee. "You heard man say, Mr. Smith own place. That all I know."

Shalagh shrugged her shoulders with a look of uncertainty feeling that Mr. Lee didn't seem to know too much about the owners.

"Well, let's see what we can find. Do you want to come with us or stay with Mr. Lee?" said Shalagh questioning the child.

Rylie decided to go with the girls, so with lantern in hand they made their way up the steep stairway. At the top of the stairs they found themselves in a narrow hallway with open doors on either side. The first door opened into a small bedroom with a slanted roof. It held a single bed covered with a white spread. A small writing table and two small windows each with frilly laced curtains adorned the room.

"I like this room. This might be mine," said Rylie hopefully touching her fingers to the flowered wallpaper.

With further investigation they discovered four more bedrooms each larger than the first and all generously furnished. At the end of the hall was a fifth room furnished in a masculine décor. Although they did not enter the room, the lamplight disclosed its contents. It held a large wooden bed and heavy appearing desk and chest of drawers. Men's attire hung in an open closet at the far end of the room. Large windows draped with thick curtains took up almost one whole wall, where a picture of a young woman was displayed on the desk. It was no one they had ever seen before. Suddenly a drape fluttered out from the window causing Tara to scream and jump back in fright.

"It's just the wind," soothed Shalagh. "Someone left the window part way open. A breeze has come up. It looks as if it might rain. I think I saw lightning off in the distance," commented Shalagh peering out into the dark cloudy night. "Perhaps I should close the window."

Not wanting to enter the privacy of some ones' room, Shalagh simply reached over and shut the door.

"I hope the owner returns tonight," she said. "I feel like an intruder in this Will Smiths' home."

"So do I," agreed Tara. "I think we've seen all there is to see. Let's go down stairs and see if Mr. Lee has finished cooking dinner. I am famished."

"Sounds good to me," said Shalagh. "I'm surely glad that Mr. Lee is with us."

Dinner was ready when they returned to the kitchen, which was warm and cozy from the heat of the cook stove. They sat around the large round kitchen table in the lamplight and greatly enjoyed Mr. Lees' delicious dinner.

"Look, Tara," said Shalagh, "Rylie is asleep in her chair.

Rylie was fast asleep with her head on her arms on the table.

"Did you find sleeping room?" questioned Mr. Lee. "Me will carry missy Rylie to her room."

"Yes, I think we will take the large room near the top of the stairs," said Shalagh. "Is that all right with you Tara it held a good sized bed or perhaps you would take a room of your own," suggested Shalagh.

"No, no, that will be fine," stated Tara pushing away from the table. "This house is a little overwhelming tonight. Perhaps tomorrow I will take my own room, but not tonight."

Mr. Lee gently picked up the sleeping child and followed the girls to the room they had chosen.

"I'm tired enough to join her," yawned Tara. "It has been a long day."

"Why don't you," suggested Shalagh. "Mr. Lee and I will bring up the suitcases. It will be better for Rylie if she were not left alone."

The child hardly stirred as the girls tucked her between the covers. The evening had grown cool. Before Shalagh could get back downstairs to help Mr. Lee with the luggage he had gone and returned bringing the suitcases with him.

"Thank you, Mr. Lee," expressed Shalagh helping him put the cases down on the floor. "I will come and help you straighten the kitchen."

"No need, missy Shalagh," explained Mr. Lee. "Me do dishes and put away while you girls talk at table."

"We're sorry, Mr. Lee, you must be tired also," lamented Tara.

"No, me fine. But could use good nights rest," he replied.

"Why don't you take the small room right at the top of the stairs Mr. Lee? I think we would feel much more comfortable if you were on this floor with us," Shalagh suggested.

"That be fine," smiled Mr. Lee in agreement. "Me lock up and turn off lamps. Good night," he said as he left the room.

"Thank you again, Mr. Lee," called Shalagh after him.

The bed was soft and the girls slept undisturbed throughout the night. They were unaware of the noise of thunder and the flashes of lightning or the lashing of the wind outside. They slept soundly and awoke in the morning with sunlight shining brightly upon them.

"Oh, it is a beautiful day," declared Rylie with excitement as she climbed over Tara, jumped out of bed and hurried to the window. "Look, look, I can see the colts. I love them already," she screamed in delight. "May we go and see them please," she begged.

"Yes, yes, I'm sure we can," Shalagh assured the child. "But we must get dressed and have breakfast first."

"Oh, let's hurry," said Rylie, "I love it here. I wonder if Mr. Lee is up. May I go and see."

"Not until your face is washed, your hair combed and you dress yourself," stated Shalagh with firmness.

"I slept so well," declared Tara stretching her arms high above her dark hair. "This reminds me of our room at Ballymore."

"I was thinking the same thing," remarked Shalagh as she brushed Rylies' hair. "The sound of the horses whinnying in the pasture and the sun streaming in the window makes me think that the cook is in the kitchen and we are ready to go down to breakfast with the family," she sighed wistfully.

"Oh, look, fresh roses on the night stand by our bed. How lovely," observed Tara. "I didn't see them last night," she declared as she stood and leaned over the pink petals taking in their perfumed odor with delight. "Oh the fragrance is heavenly as if they were fresh picked."

"They are fresh. They are wet," disclosed Shalagh as she touched the soft velvety petals. "I don't remember that vase of flowers last night either."

"I'm sure they must have been here." assumed Tara. "Perhaps there is a leak in the ceiling," she laughed. "I thought I heard it raining in the night."

The matter of the flowers was put aside as the girls busied themselves straightening the room and dressing.

"Last one down to the kitchen has to cook," yelled Tara as she took off down the hallway toward the stairs.

This brought Shalagh and Rylie quickly following behind her. They found that Mr. Lee had been up for some time. He greeted them with a cheery hello as they entered the kitchen.

"Come right in ladies," he invited as he smiled his gracious smile. "Food already. Nice place this farm. Plenty eggs in hen house. But, no find cows for milk, only horses. Very pretty, but no give milk."

The table was set for three. Bacon and eggs sat in a covered warmer on the back of the stove. Fresh baked muffins warm from the oven had been placed on a dainty covered tray on the table. Hot coffee bubbled on the stove, sending its aroma throughout the sunny kitchen. In the center of the table was a bouquet of fresh cut roses, still wet from the rain.

"Sit down ladies, or food get cold," urged Mr. Lee.

They didn't have to be coaxed. Everything looked too good to pass up.

"Mr. Lee, please join us," invited Shalagh.

"No, no, Mr. Lee already have breakfast while girls sleep. You go ahead and enjoy," he answered. "Me stir up cake for later. Then maybe I should go," he smiled rather wistfully. "Nice kitchen. Good house. Mr. Lee like it fine," he added as he briskly stirred the cake batter in a big bowl and added flour from the pantry.

"Oh, everything is delicious," complemented Tara.

"It's surely is," agreed Shalagh. "I can't help wondering though when Mr. Smith, or whoever lives here will return. It would seem they must come and care for the horses soon."

"Maybe not," acknowledged Mr. Lee. "Horses are in good pasture—lots of water in tank from windmill. Person could stay away for some days."

"What about the chickens?" questioned Rylie between bites of food.

"Chickens free to come and go. Take care of selves," Mr. Lee explained as he bent and placed the filled cake pans into the heated oven.

"Maybe no one lives here," offered Shalagh in jest. "Perhaps this is our farm and we will never know who our benefactor is."

"That would be just dreadful," sighed Tara. "Why, we don't know the first thing about how to run a farm. Why would anyone do such as thing as that."

"Let's not worry about it Tara. I am sure whoever owns the farm will return soon. By the way," she added, "did you put fresh flowers in our room this morning, Mr. Lee?"

"No do, missy Shalagh," stated Mr. Lee. "Put fresh flowers on table in kitchen, but sorry, no think to put fresh flowers in girl's room," he explained. "If you want flowers in room, I put them there after while, OK?"

"No, no that is quite all right," replied Shalagh realizing that Mr. Lee knew nothing about the flowers in their room.

After breakfast, they had morning prayers around the table with Mr. Lee joining them. With prayers over, Rylie could wait no longer to visit the horses and see the farm. She ran carefree from one thing to another. She adored the colts and horses and named the two younger colts, Pitty and Patty, after the goats aboard the Christiana.

"Rylie, the colts may already have names. I am sure whoever owns these colts will not appreciate the names you have given them," Shalagh tried to explain to the child.

"But, I miss Pitty and Patty," replied Rylie holding a fat blade of grass up to the nostril of a frisky colt.

He snorted and took a sudden jump backward and then several bouncy leaps into the air. Rylie laughed merrily at the colts' lively show of antics.

Later the girls picked wildflowers along the path that led into the thick woods. After walking a short distance along a mossy trail under the trees they came upon a wild blackberry patch. They picked and ate of the tempting fruit, while wandering further into the woods. The sound and sight of the brilliant blue lake water lapping against the shore through the trees was captivating. With giggles and gleeful anticipation they cleared the woods and slipped and slid down the sandy incline to the water below. Here they pulled off their shoes and waded and splashed in delight in the cool refreshing water.

"It looks like the ocean, doesn't it" remarked Tara, "Almost like being home in Ireland."

"Yes, somehow the sight of the water brings comfort to me," agreed Shalagh, "I feel closer to those we have lost, even though we are quite alone here."

"Except for Mr. Lee," said Rylie.

"I wish Mr. Lee could stay with us permanently," said Tara wishfully. "It just feels good having him around."

"Me too," agreed Rylie, "I love him and he cooks so good." Rylie was covered with purple berry stains on her hands and cheeks. The cold lake water had not removed them.

"That would be wonderful," agreed Shalagh. "You know, I think it must be near noon," she said cupping her hands over her eyes attempting to stare up through the green trees toward the sun. "The sun is about over our heads. We should go back. Mr. Lee may worry about us," said Shalagh with concern.

They sauntered slowly back in the direction from which they had come attempting to wipe berry stains from their hands by rubbing them together.

"The berries were good, but I think I ate too many," confessed Tara holding her stomach.

"Are you sick?" asked Shalagh with an immediate concern.

"No, but they were good," laughed Tara.

Rylie had run on ahead and now she came skipping back toward them.

"There is a lady up the path away," she declared breathlessly.

"A-a lady," stuttered Shalagh, "where?"

"She was right there at the edge of the woods," Rylie assured them pointing in the direction from which she came. "She had on a blue dress and a big straw hat."

"Did-did she talk to you?" stammered Tara as they cleared the woods and started across open ground toward the house.

"No, she was facing the other way. I don't think she saw me," explained the child.

"Well, she's gone now, unless she went into the house or stable," assumed Shalagh scanning the area.

A quick search of the stable revealed no one.

"I wonder if she lives in the house across the road," mused Tara.

"That could be," agreed Shalagh. "We will go over and introduce ourselves this afternoon. She may be able to tell us who our benefactors are."

Mr. Lee greeted them happily as they entered the kitchen.

"Lunch all on table. Fine selection of food in pantry. I have very good time in lovely kitchen while girls walk in woods. You find berries?" he laughed catching a glimpse of Rylies' hands and face.

"Yes, we could not stop picking and eating them," said Tara.

"You should bring some to Mr. Lee and I make pie. Except I leave today, so no make pie," stated Mr. Lee sadly.

The girls washed up with water from the pump by the back porch. Mr. Lee brought them a towel.

"I suppose it would be too much for us ask you to stay on for a few more days," inquired Shalagh of Mr. Lee as she dried her hands on the towel he offered.

"Yes, at least until our benefactors arrive," added Tara.

"Please, please, Mr. Lee," chimed in Rylie. "We want very much for you to stay."

Mr. Lee looked surprised but very pleased. He was silent for a moment in deep thought.

"I stay bit longer," he replied, "if girls need me."

"Oh, we do," said Shalagh with a sigh of relief. "I will write a letter immediately to Annabelle and explain that you will be staying for awhile. I'm sure she will understand."

"Mr. Lee did you see a woman come out of the woods ahead of us?" questioned Shalagh as they all sat down for lunch.

"No, me see no woman. But, Mr. Lee busy in kitchen," he explained. "You see woman in woods?"

"Rylie did," Shalagh offered, "but, she was gone by the time we arrived back here. Perhaps she lives across the road."

"Could be," agreed Mr. Lee.

"We will go over after lunch and call on her," stated Shalagh.

They all nodded in agreement.

Chapter Nineteen

The visit to the house across the road was uneventful. No one came in response to their persistent rapping on the back door.

"Well, there is no one here," declared Shalagh.

"Whoever lives here may have gone into the village," suggested Tara. "It's a pretty little house. I like having people living so close by."

"Yes, and I am glad the village is not far away," said Shalagh. "We can walk for supplies or to the shops."

"It will be convenient," agreed Tara. "But have you ever seen so many trees," she asked as they crossed the road and returned to the farm.

"Except for the lake and cleared ground, we are certainly surrounded by forrest," stated Shalagh. "It would be easy to get lost."

"Don't you go into the woods alone," shouted Tara to Rylie as the child skipped off to pet the colts.

"I won't she responded," with a quick glance back at Tara.

Rylies' hair had grown to a more attractive length, now, although still very short. It fell softly about her face giving here an angelic appearance. The only time she spoke of the past was to repeat the incident of how Jesus had come to visit her in the workhouse.

"She's such an angel child," commented Tara, "both in appearance and actions. How I wish Aunt Hala could have lived to see her."

"I think she can," disclosed Shalagh. "Perhaps they are all looking down on us from heaven."

"She has never forgotten about seeing Jesus when she was in the workhouse," remarked Tara.

"Yes, and she loves him very much. She has a much deeper understanding of the things of God than most children," said Shalagh.

"I think more so than most adults," added Tara. "She amazes me sometimes."

"Well, she has been through some great trials and thankfully she has learned to put her trust in her beloved Jesus," agreed Shalagh. "She saw him and believed he would take care of her and he has."

The afternoon passed swiftly. They walked about the farm finding much to see including a well cared for vegetable garden on one side of the house.

"Someone really takes a great deal of pride in this place," observed Tara. "Look at the neat rows of vegetables and flowers," she pointed out.

"Yes, and I wonder who and where they could be," sighed Shalagh with a pensive look. "There are no weeds in the garden. Some one is caring for it on a regular basis."

They spent a happy afternoon strolling about Rose Cottage farm and enjoyed wading again in the cool lake water. Mr. Lee prepared a splendid supper that evening and later the girls helped him with the dishes. Finally, they all sat together on the porch. They talked until well after dark. It was a comfortable place, crickets chirping and the creaking of the porch swing with the sound of water as the waves rolled gently against the shore.

"I wish Mr. Smith would come home," said Tara with her arm protectively around Rylie who was seated beside her enjoying the swaying of the swing.

"Yes, I hope they won't be upset that we are here enjoying their hospitality, but, this is where our journey ended," stated Shalagh.

"This right place, me sure," said Mr. Lee assuredly with a nod of his head. "Mr. Lee's instructions say come here. Mr. Lee not make mistake. Mr. Smith come home soon. Maybe tomorrow or maybe tonight."

"Well, we trust you are right, Mr. Lee," said Shalagh apprehensively. "It is a beautiful place, but I would feel much better if this mystery of who owns it and why we are here was solved."

"So would I," agreed Tara. "I never heard of a Mr. Smith. I wonder where Caleb and Dylan are right now," meditated Tara.

"Mr. Smith be friend of Captain, probably," explained Mr. Lee. "That why he send you here, no mystery."

"That could be, but I don't know why Captain Logan would be that concerned about our safety and well being," questioned Shalagh. "Some one certainly is paying for our expenses and care. That is a mystery."

"Guess so," agreed Mr. Lee. "Maybe we find answers tomorrow," he yawned.

"Are we keeping you up, Mr. Lee?" asked Tara. She knew that Mr. Lee liked to retire early and rise early.

"I think we all should get some rest," declared Shalagh, "and perhaps tomorrow will provide some answers to our questions."

"It is so nice out her on the porch," sighed Tara, "but I think I just got bit by one of those pesky bugs. Mosquito or whatever you call them. Oh, there is another one she squealed."

She and Rylie jumped from the swing and scurried to the door with Shalagh and Mr. Lee close behind them. Mr. Lee lit a lamp in the kitchen, explaining that he was very tired and would they mind if he retired for the night. They all agreed that was a good idea. Mr. Lee again took the small room at the top of the stairs and the girls went on to their room closing the door behind them.

It was nearly morning when Shalagh suddenly woke from a deep sleep. She had been dreaming pleasant dreams of family and home. It was very dark and all was quiet. Yet, she sensed something unusual-a lingering presence of some one or something close by. Perhaps it was the memory of her dream that would not leave her. The air was heavy with the fragrance of fresh roses. She reached with her fingers toward the table beside the bed. She felt the soft velvet petals of roses again. She knew that they had not been there when they retired for the evening.

"Did you hear that?" questioned Tara in a soft but alarming tone of voice, as she set up in bed now fully awake.

"I don't know," answered Shalagh softly, now cautiously sliding out of bed. "I just have this eerie feeling that some one besides us has been in this room."

"Oh, you are scaring me," whispered Tara as she shivered at the thought of an intruder.

"Me too," whimpered Rylie who was also very much awake. She slid down under the covers while pulling them over her head.

"I thought I heard someone moaning, or crying, or something," said Tara softly. "Listen, I think I hear it again."

Shalagh strained to listen but not for long as a soft mournful cry suddenly came from somewhere down the hall. The lamenting sobs were filled with great poignancy and turmoil. Then what had begun as a soft whimper now rose to a shrill wailing cry. The sound seemed to come from the far end of the hall in the direction of the largest bedroom. Now, frozen in fear the girls waited transfixed unable to move. Then all was silent and the darkness shrouded them with terror.

"Wh-where is it coming from?" stammered Shalagh regaining some courage and composure as the silence continued.

"I-I think it's coming from the far end of the hall where the large bedroom is situated," returned Tara in a very hushed tone of voice. "Oh, no, look, our door is open and it, it's, whatever it is, is moving toward us. It's some kind of bright light coming toward us from down the hall," gasped Tara, who was no longer whispering.

"I, I see it," groaned Shalagh falling back against the bed, her heart pounding wildly. "What shall we do?"

A fluttering beacon of light now glided slowly toward the open bedroom door. Shalagh knew she had closed the door when they retired for the night.

"Who, who is there?" questioned Shalagh in a barely audible voice. "Is that you Mr. Lee?" she pleaded.

"It could be Mr. Lee," murmured Tara as the wavering glow moved closer. "Perhaps he walks in his sl-sleep," stuttered Tara. "But, I guess not," she groaned clutching Shalaghs' gown as the silent figure of a woman now appeared directly in front of the open door.

The apparition stood motionless just outside of the doorway. Small of frame, she was clad in a blue skirt and a long sleeved white blouse. Her features were concealed by the brightly, lighted lantern, which she held tightly in an uplifted hand. In her other hand she clutched a bouquet of roses by the stems. She took a step into the room and then backed away. Then in a swift flowing motion she moved silently in the direction of the stairway. Somewhere near the stairs or on them she began to moan a grievous sound and to weep uncontrollably. The light disappeared and all was silent leaving the air heavy with the scent of roses.

For a few seconds the girls were unable to move and then Shalagh stood up unsteadily.

"Who or what on earth was that?" gasped Shalagh, now taking deep breaths of air.

"I do not know," answered Tara, "but I think it might have been a spirit or ghost that Papa used to talk about. This house may be haunted," she shivered. "It's called Rose Cottage and she carried roses."

Just then somewhere below a door slammed with a loud reverberating sound.

"I think our ghost has gone out of the kitchen door," conveyed Shalagh attempting to gather her wits about herself. "I don't believe it is a ghost. I think that it is a person and where is Mr. Lee," she questioned. "How could he sleep through all of this?"

"He was really tired last night," offered Tara as she slipped out of bed and crossed over to a window as the first rays of morning light moved into the room. "Perhaps it was just a nightmare," she weakly suggested.

"I had a dream," Rylie informed them gingerly pushing the covers from off of her head. I dreamed a woman was standing over our bed looking at us."

"Are you sure it was a dream?" asked Shalagh with increased interest as she sat down on the edge of the bed while putting her arms around the frightened child.

"Yes, yes, I am sure, because when I looked again there was no one there," explained Rylie. "I, I thought it was my Momma."

"There, there she is in the yard!" yelled Tara. "She's walking toward the woods."

Tara pointed in excitement toward the moving figure below. Shalagh and Rylie jumped from the bed and ran to the window just in time to see the flickering light of a lantern move off into the trees at the edge of the deep woods disappearing quickly from view.

"Well, whoever it was, is gone for now," stated Shalagh with a heavy sigh of relief.

"Yes, but what is to keep her from returning?" asked Tara shaking her head with dismay.

"You are right," agreed Shalagh. "Let's find Mr. Lee."

In one accord the girls dashed quickly down the hall to Mr. Lee's room. They didn't rap but pounded and screamed until Mr. Lee opened the door.

"What, what wrong?" questioned Mr. Lee rubbing his eyes attempting to make some sense of the jumbled words they were trying to speak.

No he had not seen or heard anyone. He had slept soundly until awakened by the pounding on his door by the girls.

"Let us dress quickly and go kitchen and calm down," suggested Mr. Lee. "then we talk while me make breakfast."

The girls obediently did as he requested. Although not in any mood for breakfast they nevertheless followed Mr. Lee down the stairs into the kitchen chattering loudly all the way.

Chapter Twenty

Mr. Lee fussed and scurried about the kitchen, starting a fire in the cook stove and listening at the same time as the girls related the events of what they had just experienced. He had not seen or heard anything in the night.

"Mr. Lee no likes spooks," he stated shaking his head.

"I don't believe it was spooks," said Shalagh. "But it is possible that this woman whoever she is could be insane and dangerous."

"Oh Shalagh, I'm frightened," gasped Tara. "I think we should go immediately to the village. What would we do if she returns?"

Shalagh and Tara had seated themselves at the kitchen table with Rylie between them. Rylie didn't seem to be upset in fact she eagerly accepted the breakfast that Mr. Lee brought to her. The sun had risen in the eastern sky and cast a mirror pink and lavender image of color across calm surface of the transient still waters of Lake Huron. Birds were awakening in the trees all along the shore and through the woods with melodious chirping. All appeared peaceful now as Mr. Lee poured coffee into two large cups and placed them on the table. As he turned to return the coffeepot back to the stove a scuffling sound was heard on the porch.

"What was that?" whispered Tara softly.

All eyes turned toward the kitchen door.

"Is, is the door bolted?" questioned Shalagh with trembling voice.

"Yes," whispered Mr. Lee putting his fingers to his lips. "I locked it when we came into the kitchen this morning. Guess we forget to bolt it last night."

He sat the coffeepot down on the stove and picked up a heavy iron frying pan. Another shuffling sound was heard and the door handle turned.

"Oh no, she is back," murmured Tara.

Now an unmistakable sound of moaning came from the area of the porch. Then a loud knocking sound was heard against the outside of the door.

"What shall we do?" anguished Shalagh, too afraid to move from her chair. Tara and Rylie had quickly moved from their chairs to stand on the other side of Mr. Lee. Then without warning a shout came from outside of the door.

"Open this door right now! It's Dylan and Caleb," shouted the voice. "We haven't got time for your stupid pranks. Caleb is hurt. Come on and open the door or I'll break the window."

For a stunned moment there was no movement. Then suddenly both Shalagh and Tara both rushed to open the door at the same time.

"Dylan, Dylan, oh it is Dylan," screeched the girls quickly running to unlock the door.

"Oh Dylan, you have grown so tall," observed Shalagh with excitement as both girls embraced the boy with hugs and kisses.

Dylan was now taller than either of his sisters and his appearance was rugged and strong.

"You have finally come," shouted Dylan with great excitement while catching both girls in his muscular arms.

They laughed and cried simultaneously together. "How long have you been here," he questioned holding them at arms' length to see them better.

"We came yesterday," answered Tara. "No, no it was the day before that. I don't know but it is so wonderful to see you," and Tara began to cry again unable to hold back her tears of joy.

"You look so well, sweet Tara," observed Dylan, "and you Shalagh, why I have never seen either of you looking more beautiful. But, who is the little girl and the gentleman with the frying pay," he questioned.

"This is Mr. Lee. He has been with us for sometime now and is a very dear friend," explained Shalagh. "The child is our cousin, Rylie. But, Dylan, where is Caleb," interrupted Shalagh. "You said he was hurt."

"Oh, how stupid of me," confessed Dylan. "In all of the excitement I left him on the porch. He took a terrible fall in the woods and I think his leg is broken."

By this time Caleb had crawled almost to the doorway. They all reached his side at the same time. He was overjoyed to see his sisters but it was evident he was in great pain.

"He's pretty bad off," stated Dylan. "He keeps passing out on me. Help me get him inside and into bed."

"Where we put him?" asked Mr. Lee hurrying about in great excitement.

"We'll put him in the bedroom off the dining room," suggested Shalagh. "Tara and I will help carry him. Mr. Lee, please go and prepare the bed."

Mr. Lee dashed ahead and had the bed prepared when they brought Caleb into the room. Caleb's face was ashen and he groaned in pain as they placed him carefully upon the bed.

"We left here four days ago and traveled by boat to Desmond Village," explained Dylan. "Our purpose in going was to buy cattle at the auction. After we had completed the sale we started for home, but we missed the boat. We made a bad decision and decided to walk home through the woods. That would have been fine, except that Caleb took a bad fall and injured his leg. We have been trying for the past two days to get here."

"Oh, Dylan, he looks really bad to me," declared Tara observing the anguish in Caleb's face.

"I am quite sure his leg is broken. I tried to make a splint for it and he has hobbled all the way with my help and a wooden stick to lean on," explained Dylan.

"I, I'm all right," moaned Caleb trying to ease their concerns. "I-I'm glad just to be home with my family. It's so wonderful that we are all together again."

His voice trailed off as the room and its' objects begin to swirl around for Caleb, uncontrollably as he tried to speak. He drifted off into a half-sleep of semi-consciousness while mumbling inaudible words.

"Dylan, we are in need of a doctor," declared Shalagh kneeling down attempting to examine Caleb's leg. "I can't tell if it's broken or not, but he surely is in great pain. Is there a doctor anywhere nearby?" she asked anxiously.

"There is a doctor in Lexington," offered Dylan, "but he is for farm animals, still he might be able to set Caleb's leg. Otherwise, I will have to return to Desmond Village and it will take two days," explained Dylan.

"Oh, please go and see if he will come," begged Shalagh.

Dylan hurried immediately from the house, saddled a horse and took off at a great speed toward Lexington. Tara and Ryle scurried to bring pillows and quilts from upstairs. These they placed around Calebs' leg, attempting to make him more comfortable. The slightest movement of his leg brought forth moans as his face grimaced from excruciating pain. Mr. Lee brought cool water in a basin and with this they sponged Calebs' feverish face and arms to cool the fever. And to make matters worse he was covered with mosquito bites. Rylie hurried to help bringing more towels and whatever was needed.

The better part of two hours passed before Dylan returned with the doctor. Dylan rode his horse with all speed up the lane with the horse and buggy close behind. Mr. Lee quickly escorted Dylan and the doctor into the room where the girls were attending Caleb. Caleb roused himself, attempting to speak with slurred speech. The doctor appeared to be very young. He was tall and thin with light brown hair and piercing blue eyes. In spite of his youth and possible lack of medical knowledge, he had a commanding air about him.

"I am Dr. Adam Kenny," he greeted them as he quickly maneuvered to Calebs' side. "Are you the young lads' sisters?" he asked as he began to examine Calebs' leg.

"Yes, yes we are," answered Shalagh. "And this is Mr. Lee and our young cousin, Rylie."

"Mr. Lee, please take the girls to the kitchen and Dylan you stay with me," said the doctor. We will have a look and see what needs to be done."

The girls quietly followed Mr. Lee into the kitchen where he immediately began to prepare tea.

"It seems the good doctor is very young," said Tara shaking her head in dismay.

"Yes, it does appear so," acknowledged Shalagh. "I'm concerned about his abilities, but we haven't much choice."

They sat at the kitchen table and waited in nervous silence, sipping the cups of tea Mr. Lee had prepared for them. After a short time, Dylan came to the kitchen door requesting Mr. Lees' assistance.

"Me be right back, missies," said Mr. Lee, "Everything be fine, not to worry."

Dylan closed the kitchen door behind them. Several more minutes went by and then Caleb suddenly roared one deafening sound and all was silent again.

"What are they doing to him?" said Tara sympathetically wringing her hands together.

"I think they set his leg, Tara," explained Shalagh. "It had to be done."

"Poor Caleb," responded Rylie sadly.

It wasn't long before the kitchen door flew open and Mr. Lee entered with one of his broad smiles.

"He be all right now, ladies," Mr. Lee informed them. "Leg set and doctor giving him a sedative. Oh, oh, nearly forgot, doctor want Mr. Lee to bring water for sedative."

Mr. Lee pumped cold water filling a pitcher and returning quickly to the bedroom. Shortly thereafter, Doctor Kenny stepped into the kitchen.

"Oh, doctor, how is he?" questioned Shalagh eagerly.

"He should do well now," explained the doctor in a serious tone. "It was a clean break and it set well. He will need attention and probable a lengthy recuperation as he has also contacted a bad case of ague. However, he is young and strong and therefore I see no real problems developing. Who will oversee the medications?," questioned the young doctor looking intently at the girls and Mr. Lee.

"I-I will," stammered Shalagh.

"All right then, let me give you my instructions," offered the doctor as he began to explain what had to be done. "Do you understand?" he questioned when he had finished.

"I think so, well, I am not sure," Shalagh answered seeming somewhat confused.

"Here, I had better write them down for you," suggested Doctor Kenny taking a pad of paper from his pocket. "Do you understand the instructions now?" he asked after Shalagh had time to look them over.

"Yes, I do," nodded Shalagh.

"Good, well then I will return tomorrow and check on my patient," stated the doctor in a professional manner.

"Mr. Lee, please prepare lunch for us," requested Shalagh.

"Good doctor welcome to stay," invited Mr. Lee.

"No, thank you, but I have other calls I must make," declined the doctor. "Perhaps another time though," he smiled glancing at Shalagh.

The girls hurried to Calebs' room as the doctor left.

"How is he Dylan?" asked Shalagh.

"He is asleep," said Dylan, "and Doctor Kenny said he would probably sleep for some time."

"He already looks much better," stated Tara. "I am much relieved. Dr. Kenny looks so young. Good looking though and rather knowledgeable for a horse doctor," she added.

"Oh, I couldn't get old Doc Saunders. He was out on a case," explained Dylan. "That's what took so long. I didn't know what to do when I couldn't find Doc Saunders, then someone told me about a new doctor who just arrived in town. I had trouble finding his office and when I did, he had patients. I had to wait, but when I finally got to see him, he came right away. I rather like him."

"Yes, I think Shalagh does too," smiled Tara while glancing mischievously at her sister.

"Oh, really," questioned Dylan.

"That is not true," stated Shalagh as she straightened the covers on Calebs' bed. Well, I mean, I liked him, but, but oh, you know what I mean."

"You were so flustered you couldn't remember his instructions," giggled Tara softly.

"I was just nervous because of all that had happened," returned Shalagh.

"I don't think so," remarked Tara.

Just then Mr. Lee quietly announced that lunch was ready. It was decided that Shalagh would remain with Caleb until someone could relieve her. After lunch, Tara and Rylie tiptoed into the room to sit with Caleb. Shalagh then joined Dylan in the kitchen. Mr. Lee left stating he wanted to gather eggs, leaving the two of them alone.

Chapter Twenty-One

Dylan and Shalagh sat quietly at the kitchen table. Shalagh attempted to eat but had no appetite because of all that had happened.

"You look tired, Dylan" said Shalagh.

"I am very tired," agreed Dylan. "I haven't slept for two nights. We did try to rest for awhile as Caleb was so exhausted, but the mosquitoes were so bad that we gave up."

"You should get some rest. We'll care for Caleb," Shalagh assured him patting Dylans' hand.

"I will soon," agreed Dylan. "But there are some things I need to talk to you about before I do."

It was difficult for Shalagh to believe that this was the same boy they had last seen in Ireland eight months ago. Dylan's appearance has changed so much and he carried a confidence about himself that he did not possess before. Still his warm, caring personality had not changed.

"Yes, there is much to talk about," agreed Shalagh, "but we can do that later when you have rested."

"That is true, but I must know about Rylie. Where did you find her?" asked Dylan, "and how did you come to bring her with you?"

"Well," said Shalagh, "we were searching for you and

Caleb. The authorities had put us out of the cottage and burned it. We traveled to Derry in search for you. It was there that we found information leading us to Rylie's whereabouts at the workhouse. We were informed that the rest of her family had perished and we had no choice but to bring her with us."

"Not all of her family has perished," Dylan informed her. "That is why it is important that I speak with you. Aunt Hala is here with us."

"Aunt Hala is alive and living here on this farm?" questioned Shalagh in absolute astonishment.

"Yes, she is," confirmed Dylan. "But her mind is very troubled. At times she appears quite normal, but at other times she is very disturbed."

"Oh, dear Aunt Hala," anguished Shalagh. "In what way is she so troubled?"

"Well, she sometimes she is fine. She knows Caleb and me and is quite rational." Continued Dylan as his voice trailed off as if in deep thought.

"Yes, go on," requested Shalagh, "what does she do?"

"For one thing, she wanders. We left here with a family in Lexington while we went to buy the cattle," said Dylan. "I hope she didn't have any of her spells while there, or cause them any trouble."

"What kind of spells?" asked Shalagh with compassionate concern,.

"Strange spells," answered Dylan, "she cries and moans and stares right through you as though you were not there at all. We don't want to put her away someplace, but it is hard. She will seem all right and before you know it she will snap and take off somewhere."

"Oh, Dylan, that would explain the woman we saw last night. She frightened us nearly out of our wits," related Shalagh. "We thought the house was haunted."

"Oh, no, she must have wandered away from the people who were caring for her. It had to be Aunt Hala," stated Dylan. "That is what she does. She has done that to Caleb and me so many times. She wakes us up in the middle of the night, moaning and carrying on."

"If these people in Lexington understood about her condition you would think they would have watched her more closely," declared Shalagh.

"Oh, she is clever and hard to figure," said Dylan. "Well, I will have to go into Lexington today and I will find her. Although, witnessing her actions, I would say she is close by, especially if you saw her last night."

"Poor little Rylie," sighed Shalagh.

"Well, it may work out better than we think," reasoned Dylan rubbing his tired eyes. "Maybe Aunt Hala will come out of it when she sees Rylie."

"I don't know how Rylie will react," declared Shalagh. "I hope it won't be too much for her."

"So you found Rylie and brought her with you," reflected Dylan. "You know that our Uncle Rudgers is behind all of this?"

"I thought he was dead a long time ago," said Shalagh.

"Everyone did," stated Dylan. "Caleb and I stayed in London for a short time, settling business and searching for you girls. It was there we spoke to Papas' attorney and found out to much of our surprise that Rudgers was very much alive. We all know the story of how he was angry when Grampa Frizzle married shortly after the death of his first wife, Rudgers mother. Until that time he was a spoiled, only child. He was filled with hate when Uncle Will was born. He despised everyone and ran off at the age of fourteen, never to be seen again."

"Until now," stated Shalagh. "Yes, that is the story that was always told about him." Didn't grandpa trace him to a ship that was lost at sea?"

"Yes, he did, but it seems now that Uncle Rudgers' life was spared. He was terribly burned in a fire aboard the ship," recalled Dylan.

"How awful," responded Shalagh, "but, where has he been all these years?"

"I don't know, but either he or some one pretending to be him, has returned with great vengeance," related Dylan. "He intends to own the linen mills and he and for a while he possessed Ballymore. I understand that he has a great knowledge of business and has applied his crafty thievery toward everything the family owns. He has retained high paid attorneys' who will stop at nothing to achieve his vindictive goals.

"Did he murder poor Papa and Uncle Will," demanded Shalagh with an expression of great sadness.

"We believe that he had them killed and by doing so destroyed everything our family has held dear," related Dylan. "He was successful in obtaining Ballymore. It seems that Papa had invested heavily in some unwise business venture somewhere in England. Papas' lawyers were much against it. It was a hoax fabricated by none other than Rudgers Pierce. Papa used Ballymore as collateral."

"So Ballymore fell into Rodgers Pierces' hands," lamented Shalagh.

"Yes, but he didn't keep it long. Bad help and a terrible economy forced Ballymore into the hands of the Bank of England," Dylan related.

"It was the Bank of England that had us removed from the Shepherds' cottage the day after you left," explained Shalagh.

"So, there would have been no one there had we returned,"

214

noted Dylan. "Because of Mr. Harcroft's death it was impossible for us to come back. The constable was sure that Caleb was a murderer and a thief."

"Who do you think murdered Mr. Harcroft?" questioned Shalagh.

"I am sure it was one or more of the help. The cash box was empty. I believe that they took the money. I know it wasn't Caleb," revealed Dylan.

"Where did you go after you left that night?" quizzed Shalagh trying to put together the pieces of the puzzle that had plagued their lives for several months.

"We went straight to Uncle Wills," related Dylan. "Someone came to the door and told us that Uncle Will was dead and Aunt Hala was in prison. They gave us no information as to Brin or Rylie's whereabouts."

"How were you able to get Aunt Hala out of prison?" inquired Shalagh.

"We bought her way out," recounted Dylan, "along with purchasing tickets for you girls aboard the Christiana."

"But, how did you accomplish all of this," asked Shalagh in amazement.

"You remember that old mantle clock of Grandma Boyd's?" inquired Dylan.

"Yes, it always sat on top of the bookcase in Papas' study. Caleb was very fond of it," remembered Shalagh.

"He likes it a lot better now," smiled Dylan. "That antique clock has been hiding grandmas' precious jewels all these years. Caleb found them the night we left for Derry."

"So the story was true, she really did hide those jewels. They must have been of great value," asserted Shalagh.

"Yes, Shalagh, they were worth a fortune. With part of those jewels we paid for all of our passages to America. We bought the farm sight unseen and still have plenty left. We don't need the linen mills or anything else that remains in Ireland."

Dylans' head drooped toward the table. Shalagh realized that he could hardly keep his head up or his eyes opened.

"Dylan, please rest for awhile," pleaded Shalagh. "You need to sleep. We can talk later."

"I have to stay awake," yawned Dylan shaking his head, trying to keep awake. "The cattle we purchased at auction are due to arrive at about four o'clock this afternoon. They are coming by boat to Lexington. We should have waited and traveled back with them, but Caleb was worried about Aunt Hala. We walked over twenty miles through woods and swamp."

"It is only a little after one, so you go up and rest awhile. I will call you in an hour or so," Shalagh insisted pulling him from the chair and directing him toward the stairway.

"So good to have you here," smiled Dylan reaching out to take hold of her hand. "I believe I will take your advice. One more thing, do you think you could help me drive the cows home from Lexington?"

"Of course I will," affirmed Shalagh. "Now, go and get some rest."

"There are twenty cows and five calves," declared Dylan. "Think we will be able to handle them?"

"Sure we can," Shalagh assured him as a great feeling of serenity filled her heart as Dylan ascended the stairs.

Yes, it was almost like home. True there were problems to solve, but they were together again as a family.

Chapter Twenty-Two

Caleb was watched over with tender care throughout the afternoon into the evening. As the day wore on the weather became extremely hot. The windows were opened wide, but there was little breeze if any. Like a glass mirror the lake beyond lay still. The girls took turns fanning Caleb and placing cool wet cloths on his feverish forehead. Shalagh was true to her word and woke Dylan at close to three o'clock.

"Are we taking the horses?" questioned Shalagh as she and Dylan left the house together.

"No, I am afraid they might scare the cattle. They are probably all ready spooked having traveled by boat so far. We will walk."

"I have never felt such heat," stated Shalagh wiping her forehead with her hand, "and what is that odor? Smells like burning wood."

"It is hot," agreed Dylan, "but, on top of that, the humidity is so high, that it makes you feel like you are in the tropics. That odor of burning is coming from the lumber mills not too far away. They cut the timber and burn the useless branches and limbs."

"The weather was so lovely when we arrived here," stated Shalagh.

"Yes, it is very changeable," replied Dylan. "I just hope the wind doesn't come up from the west. An east wind is good, sending cool breezes across Lake Huron. A wind out of the west could be trouble on a hot day like this. There have been quite a few fires not far from us. People are careless about burning off their fields."

"With all of these woods, that could be very dangerous," agreed Shalagh.

Even with the shade from the many trees, the walk into Lexington was stifling.

"You bought the farm, sight unseen," questioned Shalagh attempting conversation in spite of the heat.

"Yes, pa's attorney had a friend who had returned to England because his wife had become ill. Her health did not permit them to come back to America and he wanted his farm sold immediately. The attorney took care of everything for us."

"When did you leave for America?" asked Shalagh.

"Well, I stayed with Aunt Hala in England while Caleb returned to Ireland in search for you girls. He could not find you and it was much to dangerous for him to remain there. Thankfully we met Captain Logan who had done business with papa in the past. He offered to help find you. Caleb worked out all of the details with the captain. He paid Captain Logan in advance for all of your expenses as estimated by Captain Logan. We arrived here in May and the land is everything it was promised to be. I will never go back to Ireland," vowed Dylan.

"Nor, I," agreed Shalagh.

The cattle had been taken off the barge and were being held in a fenced enclosure near the dock when Dylan and Shalagh arrived in Lexington. Shalagh was sure she would like Lexington. It appeared to be a quiet village with small shops in a peaceful setting. Today, however, it was too hot to enjoy. The wind that Dylan had feared came up suddenly out of the west and was beginning to blow up a storm. The cattle were restless and agitated by the oncoming storm and the uncertainty of their situation.

"I wanted to stop and check on Aunt Halas' possible whereabouts," yelled Dylan over the increasing sound of the wind. "I'll come back afterwards, when we get the cows home. Aunt Hala is probably not there anyway and will show up on her own."

"I'm glad we don't have to take them too far," shouted Shalagh. "It sounds like a gale is blowing in."

"Come on, we haven't a moment to lose. Let's start moving them toward home," hollered Dylan. "We can't keep them here. Let's hope the worst holds off until we get there."

The fierce blowing wind picked up the beach sand and blew it into their faces. Thunder rumbled nearby. Quickly they released the cattle from the enclosure and begin to drive them toward the farm. Conversation was limited and was directed at the cattle in an attempt to keep them together and moving in the right direction. They moved along swiftly, probably relieved to be free from the boat and on solid ground again.

"I think we are going to make it," Shalagh, "we are almost home," shouted Dylan after sometime of maneuvering the stock along the road.

Just at that moment a tree came crashing down in the woods beside of the road. Shalagh and Dylan fought hard to calm the cattle and keep them from running off in all directions. One frightened calf broke into a gallop and started through the thick underbrush.

"Keep them moving ahead, Shalagh, I have to get that calf," yelled Dylan over the sound of the wind.

Dylan took off into the woods.

"Keep on going. Keep moving," he shouted back at Shalagh.
It was then that Shalagh saw her. She was standing in the
middle of the road. The sand and wind was whipping her skirt
and blowing her hair wildly about her face. She stood
motionless. It was the woman in the blue skirt and white blouse.
Her hat had blown away letting her hair fly loose. It was Aunt
Hala. She just stood there, frozen in fear as the cattle ran wildly
toward her. Then a flash of lightning and a loud burst of thunder
caused the cows to panic. They begin to rush headlong toward
the frail little woman. Shalagh screamed for Aunt Hala to
move, but she did not.

"Run, Aunt Hala, run," screamed Shalagh as she tried
desperately to scatter the cattle away from her.

It seemed hopeless. The cattle continued to surge straight
toward Aunt Hala. Then suddenly out of nowhere appeared Mr.
Lee. He was not a moment too soon as he quickly grabbed Aunt
Hala and pulled her from certain death just as the rampaging
cattle passed by.

Just ahead now, through the pouring rain, Shalagh saw Tara
standing at the entrance to the lane. She was wildly waving her
arms in an effort to direct the frightened cows toward the barn.
By the time Shalagh arrived at the lane, Dylan caught up with
her. He was half-carrying and half dragging the stubborn calf.
Shalagh could see that the barn door was open and in a matter
of seconds, the cows, calves and all were safely inside. Tara
slammed the barn door shut just as the storm broke in all of its
fury.

"I didn't think we were going to make it," gasped Dylan.
"Boy, this is a gully washer."

"But, Dylan," exclaimed Shalagh, "didn't you see Aunt
Hala standing in the middle of the road? She would have been
terribly hurt or worse, but Mr. Lee pulled her to safety just in
time. Do you think they are all right?"

"That woman in the road was Aunt Hala?" questioned Tara in unbelief. "What are you talking about?"

"Yes, Aunt Hala is alive and the boys brought her with them from Ireland," explained Shalagh. "They found her in a prison in Derry. She is our mysterious ghost."

"Oh, I can't believe it," cried Tara. "Aunt Hala, here with us? Mr. Lee and I heard you coming and went to help. Then, that woman, Aunt Hala suddenly came out of the woods and I guess the cows startled her. She just couldn't seem to move."

"Girls, you get the cows settled and fed," suggested Dylan, "and I will go and look for Aunt Hala and Mr. Lee.

Dylan took off into the storm again.

The cows were fed and watered and placed into individual stalls. A short time later the girls made a dash toward the back door of the kitchen, getting completely drenched in the process. Once inside they were totally amazed at what they encountered. Aunt Hala sat comfortably at the kitchen table, sipping a cup of hot tea while Mr. Lee busied himself about the kitchen.

"How is she, Mr. Lee?" questioned Shalagh softly.

"She fine. She be fine. She just need be calm down," insisted Mr. Lee.

About that time Dylan came bursting into the kitchen.

"Did you find them? Oh thank the Lord," he said realizing that Aunt Hala and Mr. Lee were safe. "Aunt Hala, you were supposed to be in Lexington," admonished Dylan. "How did you get here?"

Aunt Hala said nothing. She just sipped her tea as Mr. Lee brought her a warm shawl and slipped it over her wet shoulders. She smiled at the kindly man.

"She be all right," Mr. Lee assured them. "She just need time to work things out."

Dylan, realizing that Mr. Lee had everything under control, pulled Shalagh aside.

"Where is Rylie?" he whispered.

"I don't know," answered Shalagh with a sudden look of concern. "Mr. Lee, come here please," demanded Shalagh drawing him into the dining room and leaving Tara alone with Aunt Hala. "Where is Rylie?" she questioned with a serious tone of voice.

"I sorry to leave her, but, missy Tara and me thought she be okay in house with Mr. Caleb," explained Mr. Lee.

"It's all right that you left her here," Shalagh assured him. "That is not the problem. The lady in the kitchen is Rylie's mother and somehow we have got to tell Rylie.

"Oh, missy, that be big surprise for Rylie. Make lady happy too," said Mr. Lee nodding his head.

"Well, perhaps," declared Shalagh looking at Dylan, "which one of us gets to tell Rylie?"

Tara had followed them quietly into the room, leaving Aunt Hala alone for a while.

"We'll go together," Tara suggested.

"Mr. Lee, would you mind staying with Aunt Hala," asked Dylan. "You seem to have a calming affect upon her."

"Mr. Lee happy to stay with pretty lady," answered Mr. Lee and he promptly returned to the kitchen.

"How is Caleb?" asked Shalagh softly as she, Dylan and Tara entered the bedroom.

"He is still asleep," said the little girl looking up from where she sat comfortably in a small rocking chair. The storm didn't even bother him."

"Rylie, would you come with Tara and me," requested Shalagh. "Dylan will stay with Caleb for a while."

Rylie obediently got up and Dylan took her place in the rocking chair.

"Is something wrong?" questioned Rylie as they entered the

dining room. She could tell by the expression on their faces that something was amiss. Shalagh was not sure how long Aunt Hala would stay in the kitchen. It was expedient that Rylie be told what had happened now.

Shalagh stood behind Rylie as if to block the sudden emergence of Aunt Hala, should she enter the room.

"Rylie, your mother has been found. She is alive and well and actually she is right here with us now," explained Tara.

At first the expression on Rylie's face was completely blank and then she began to dance about.

"Oh, I am so happy," laughed Rylie, clapping her little hands together in a burst of glee. "Where is she?" asked the joyful child now looking about the room in earnest expectation. "I knew she would come, I knew she would come. Oh, where is she?" squealed Rylie now putting her hands over her mouth still attempting to be quiet so as not to awaken Caleb.

"Rylie, wait just a minute," cautioned Tara. "We haven't told your mama that you are here yet. She has been very sick and she may not recognize you."

"Jesus can make her well," declared the child still looking anxiously around the room.

"That is true," replied Tara, "but, we will let Shalagh go and explain to her that you are here and then you and I will go together to see her, all right?"

"All right," agreed Rylie her countenance flooded with joy.

"Thank you so much for giving me the job," said Shalagh looking very upset at Tara.

Mr. Lee was pouring more tea for Hala as Shalagh entered the room. Hala turned at the sound of someone approaching.

"Aunt Hala," said Shalagh stepping close to the table. "Do you know who I am?"

Hala studied Shalaghs' face for a moment. Then she looked

away as if in deep thought. Just as Shalagh became sure of receiving no reply, Hala turned toward her again. Then with a subdued sparkle in her eyes she quite wittily replied.

"Don't you know who you are?" and she laughed softly and then she responded with, "Yes, my dear, I know you. You are one of Taryns' girls. I believe you are Shalagh, the older one."

"Shalagh was very encouraged and delighted to hear Aunt Halas' answer to her question.

"Yes, yes, you are correct, I am Shalagh, Taryns oldest girl," affirmed Shalagh. "And I have a wonderful surprise for you dear one. God has brought part of your family together again. He in his mercy has gathered us from out of our grief and sorrow and placed us here to love and comfort each other. Our Heavenly Father has spared our lives and that of your little girl. Rylie is here with us and most anxious to see you."

"Rylie is here? How can that be?" questioned Aunt Hala. "They told me that all of my family were gone—that the children perished in the work house."

"Tara and I brought Rylie here from Ireland," explained Shalagh. "We found her in a work house. What they told you was not true."

Hala sat with her elbows on the table. She placed her delicate hands to her forehead and closed her eyes as tears streamed down her cheeks. Shalagh began to pray softly as she knelt down beside Halas' chair.

"I thought they were all gone," sobbed Hala now raising her head up to face Shalagh. "Will, Rylie and Bryn all gone, but you tell me that Rylie still lives? Is that true?"

Tara and Rylie had stepped into the kitchen hand in hand.

"I am here mama," spoke Rylie letting go of Taras' hand moving quickly to her mothers' side.

"Oh, my child, it is really you," gasped Hala while pulling Rylie into her arms in a joyous embrace.

"It is me, mama. Oh, I am so glad you have come!" exclaimed Rylie. "Jesus told me you would come and now you are here."

Joy flooded the room and soon everyone was talking and embracing each other all at the same time. Mr. Lee was so happy for the family that he loved so dearly he could hardly contain himself.

"You need not be afraid anymore, Miss Hala," said Mr. Lee. "Jesus be here, family be here. We take care of each other. We never be alone again."

Chapter Twenty-Three

Summer unfolded into autumn with a rush of brilliant color. Crimson, amber, purple and brown leaves in remarkably bright and varied hues graced the woods surrounding Rose Cottage Farm. Warm nights turned cool. Wild geese took their flight from the marshes along the shore in quest of warmer climates. Ripe apples, pears and plums were put up into delicious sauces, jellies and jams. Vegetables and fruits canned, dried and preserved filled the pantry shelves to overflowing. The cattle and horses fur grew thick and heavy with a lustrous sheen. Small woodland creatures scurried undauntedly while gathering and storing provisions for the winter months ahead. The wind blew stronger with gusts from the northeast, sending golden leaves in every direction until the trees were bare. The deep blue, gray waters of Lake Huron were whipped into huge rolling waves. They thundered against the shoreline and then broke, rolling the turbulent white-capped breakers back out to sea only to return crashing again and again upon the sandy beaches and rugged coastline behind Rose Cottage Farm.

Then, one breathless morning revealed an awesome beauty. Dazzling white snow covered the ground everywhere. It adorned and garnished with wintry splendor every tree bough fence and building. Over it all was a sheath of sparkling ice. The sudden storm had moved on to claim new territory, leaving behind an incredible elusion that Rose Cottage had become an ice palace in an enchanted fairyland.

The long winter months were filled with comfort and plenty. New friends and commitments were established in the village and nearby church.

As abruptly as winter had arrived it was slow to take its leave. Finally, it relinquished its' hold to the gentle coaxing of spring. Warm sunshine caressed the land and gentle rains pushed forth the blossoms on the trees and the woods gave birth to wild flowers in abundant fragrances.

Life on the quiet farm near Lexington soon unfolded into a happy contented pattern of living. The family quickly became a highly respected and influential part of the community. Rose Cottage Farm was so near the village that it gave its occupants easy access to church and social functions. Still it was far enough away to allow them solitude and privacy of life. Memories of those not with them any longer would be cherished, never forgotten, and bound forever with cords of love within their hearts.

Shalagh and Tara had made many friends among them was young Dr. Kenny who often requested Shalagh's help assisting him on his frequent house calls. Shalagh had to agree that the young doctor was quite handsome, but so serious and detached. It made her feel that nothing was important to him but the profession that he had chosen. However, she took it graciously and considered it a great learning experience as the young doctor was teaching her much about medicine. Still, he joined them in many family gatherings and always was able to find a seat beside her in church services.

Caleb had a steady girlfriend who was lovely and sweet, her name was Violet. That romance was destined to be put on hold as Caleb had been accepted to enter a large state university come the fall of the year.

Mr. Lee had decided, with the pleasant and persistent urging of the family, to make his permanent home at Rose Cottage Farm. His talent for cooking was readily accepted and enjoyed by the family as he continued to apply his skills and prepare his special dishes. He also managed the affairs of the house. He always wore his spotlessly white valet jacket and meticulously performed his duties with great pride and care. He committed himself to caring for Hala and she flourished under his attentive and diligent treatment. Although she was charitable to him, she was also commanding and demanding. He called her his little sister and treated her with the loyalty of a servant to a queen. When the dark shadows of past memories would envelope Hala's mind and she began to slip into a lonely bleakness that would take over her thoughts, Mr. Lee would gently talk to her about pleasant things. He would read from the Bible or some uplifting book of poems. Many times they would just sit at the kitchen table, Hala sipping tea and Mr. Lee reading in his broken English. If her anguish were too great or too deep, he would speak to her in consoling gentle words ever leading her to the healing light of God's word. Jesus be the Day Star, little sister, Jesus be the Day Star, was always Mr. Lee's assuring promise to calm her fears. She never again wandered away or fell into her strange spells.

Today was the first day of summer and an exciting day as Annabelle had come to visit. She had arrived in the morning causing a great stir.

"Annabelle, Annabelle," yelled the girls with great excitement as they scurried from the garden where they were hard at work.

Annabelle had previously written explaining her arrival

would be in a day or two but wasn't quite sure when. Mr. Billie brought her by wagon from the boat in Lexington. She came with a suitcase and a medium sized wooden crate. Mr. Billie placed the suitcase on the ground and then at Annalbelle's command lifted down the crate. Mr. Lee and Hala had now joined in the happy arrival of Annabelle. Caleb and Dylan were busy working in the fields.

"I brought a surprise for Rylie," laughed Annabelle pointing to the crate.

"What is it? What is it?" shouted Rylie in joyous expectation.

"Well, open it up, boy," demanded Annabelle of Mr. Billie.

Mr. Billie quickly used his tools to open the crate and soon out popped a hairy nose.

"Oh," screamed Rylie, "Oh, oh," as she danced in happy leaps about the crate.

A few more applications of his wedge bar brought down the side and out staggered a wobbly little goat followed closely by another.

"It's Pitty and Patty. Oh, I love you, I love you," squealed the happy child while trying to embrace them both at the same time.

After a few moments the goats regained the use of their legs and appeared to be as overjoyed to see Rylie and Mr. Lee and they were to see them.

"I thought the farm would be a fitt'en place for them," stated Annabelle," knowing how much Rylie loved them."

"Oh, I do love them, I do," agreed Rylie as she lovingly continued to apply kisses and hugs on her beloved pets.

Annabelle spent several days at Rose Cottage, enjoying the quiet countryside on the shore of beautiful Lake Huron. She explained more fully her involvement in the events and particulars of the journey that had brought them from Ireland to the USA and how it had been successfully secured. She confirmed that it had taken a great deal of ingenuity on the Captains' part and trusting individuals all along the way.

Annabelle was also delighted to announce the birth of her cherished grandson. She took great pleasure in explaining his exact measurements, weight and how beautiful his appearance. Surprisingly, she and Captain had sold the Christiana and purchased a home near a scenic river in Detroit. Their daughters' husband had been transferred to Detroit and Annabelle and the Captain desired to be close to them. Through the years, Annabelle would return many times, bringing with her one of her daughters or grandchildren.

Mr. Lee had been working industriously in the kitchen all morning.

"People be coming soon," he smiled as Shalagh and Tara carried the food, which he had deliciously and carefully prepared, to long tables set outside on the green lawn.

"Be careful miss Rylie, that lemonade pitcher be heavy he cautioned while giving Rylie something lighter to carry. "Watch the door not slam back on you," he warned.

Rylie managed quite well to carry a large covered tray of sandwiches to one of the outside tables.

"Oh, here comes Caleb with Violet," Rylie shouted with excitement running to meet them, "and the Jones' too."

Shalagh and Tara had decided to invite the church families and some of the towns' people to a get acquainted potluck picnic for Annabelle. Mr. Lee had himself prepared enough food for an army. As guests arrived the tables became filled to overflowing with a delicious assortment and variety of sumptuous edibles.

The sound of happy, friendly laughter gently drifted through the air as more and more guests arrived, greeting each other in delightful anticipation of an afternoon of enjoyable fellowship with friends. Shalagh and Tara after greeting each of the guests introduced them to Annabelle. Soon they were comfortably seated around the long tables and after grace was said began to partake of the delicious food.

The warm pleasant afternoon passed too quickly with Annabelle catching the boat from Lexington to Detroit at four o'clock. Most of the guests left at about the same time as Annabelle, graciously thanking their hosts for such a wonderful afternoon of pleasant fellowship and deliciously prepared food.

It was now early evening and Shalagh sat contentedly in the parlor waiting for Dr. Kenny. She was going to make a late house call with him tonight. Mr. Lee had finished the dishes and he and Aunt Hala were having a conversation about the fireplace in the same room.

"I don't think that draft is open enough," stated Aunt Hala.

"It be fine," Mr. Lee assured her.

Hala poked her head into the fireplace opening and looking up into the chimney commented.

"I noticed the other night that the draft was not drawing right," insisted Hala.

"Come away from there little sister. You get all sooty," said Mr. Lee. "Mr. Lee fix it for you tomorrow."

Tara and Dylan were playing some kind of new board game with Caleb and Violet in the dining room. The sound of their excited voices carried into the parlor.

"Will you read to me, Shalagh," asked Rylie as she squeezed in beside her in a soft overstuffed chair.

"Of course I will," replied Shalagh moving over in the chair to give Rylie a little more room. "I will read until Dr. Kenny arrives. Where is your book?"

"I'll get it," said Rylie sliding out of the chair and running into the library and sorting through the books in order to find just the right story.

Deep in thought Shalagh waited for Rylie to return. She was happy on this farm, in a new country, far from their native Ireland. She had no fear of the future, nor dread of the past. The past, although indelibly etched upon her mind-the chaotic trials and adversities were gradually being replaced by the blessed thought of a bright new future. A future wrought by God and one totally in God's hands. I have beheld God's love in marvelous ways concluded Shalagh. He has led us with his almighty hand and brought us from fear to faith and confidence. He has given us power over defeat and his matchless love to overcome grief. I have witnessed His great miracles and have trembled in His divine presence. My life is forever, touched by God and "the lines are fallen unto me in pleasant places; yea, I have a goodly heritage, yea even more than the sparrows."